Camp Club Girls

Alexis and the
LAKE TAHOE TUMULT

© 2011 by Barbour Publishing, Inc.

Edited by Jeanette Littleton.

ISBN 978-1-60260-406-3

Cover design: Thinkpen Design

Published by Barbour Publishing, Inc., P.O. Box 719, Uhrichsville, Ohio 44683, www.barbourbooks.com

Our mission is to publish and distribute inspirational products offering exceptional value and biblical encouragement to the masses.

Member of the
Evangelical Christian
Publishers Association

Printed in the United States of America.
Dickinson Press Inc., Grand Rapids, MI 49512; April 2011; D10002783

Camp Club Girls

Alexis and the
LAKE TAHOE TUMULT

Erica Rodgers

BARBOUR
PUBLISHING

Cat's Out of the Bag

"Only about twenty more minutes to the hotel!" said Mr. Howell. Alexis's dad hummed as he guided their rented car up the winding road that would take them to Lake Tahoe.

The flat, icy landscape scattered with sagebrush had turned into snowy peaks. As Alexis gazed at them, her imagination started to go wild. She decided the snowy peaks reached into the bright blue sky like the jagged teeth of a crocodile—like the crocodiles she'd seen in a documentary on the Discovery Channel earlier in the month.

And of course her thoughts of documentaries and the Discovery Channel made her think of the real purpose she and her friend Bailey, a fellow Camp Club Girl, had for going to Lake Tahoe with Alexis's mom and dad and twin brothers.

"Hey, Dad?" Alexis called. "Can we go straight to the animal reserve?"

"I don't see why not," Mr. Howell said. "It's too late to ski today, anyway. I'll drop your mom and brothers off at the hotel. They can check in and hang out while I drive you out there. We'll be back by dinner."

Alexis yawned and closed her eyes. She thought again about those big teeth on the crocodiles.

Suddenly the car began to swerve and shake as if those crocodile teeth had gotten hold of the Howells' car.

"What's going on?" asked Mrs. Howell.

"Not sure!" said Mr. Howell. He was struggling to keep his hands on the steering wheel. Alexis looked out the window and realized that the car wasn't all that was shaking.

"Dad, is this an earthquake?" she asked.

Mr. Howell didn't answer. He was focused on dodging the rocks that had begun rolling down the hill above them.

But almost as suddenly as the bouncing of the earth had begun, it stopped. Within a matter of minutes, the car was driving smoothly again.

"What a way to start a vacation, huh?" Mr. Howell laughed nervously. "I think that *was* a small earthquake."

Alexis turned to Bailey, but her fellow Camp Club Girl was fast asleep, face pressed against the window.

The breath from her gaping mouth was fogging the glass. Alexis peeked into the back of the van where her little brothers were also sleeping.

There was no way Alexis could have slept, even before the earthquake. She was too excited about her documentary.

The owners at the Tahoe Animal Reserve and Rescue at Lake Tahoe had agreed to let her tour and film their facilities. Her video would be about remembering nature in the middle of our world full of cement and SUVs.

She was planning to enter the video in a contest for young amateur filmmakers. The winner of the contest would not only see the film shown on the Discovery Channel but would also receive scholarship money. And knowing how much her mother's youngest sister was still paying on loans she'd taken out for college, Alexis knew it was never too early to start saving money for college!

So even though she was only twelve, Alex, as most of her friends called her, was going to get started. She loved movies. She knew when she grew up, she wanted to work with films in some way, perhaps as a director. She'd lived in Sacramento all her life and knew of several good colleges that offered classes to prepare students for the film industry.

Since she loved to operate a camera, Alexis was very excited to enter the contest.

And what better place to record nature than in Lake Tahoe? From the time pioneers had discovered the lake in 1844, it had been a tourist attraction. People from all around the world visited the area to enjoy its beauty.

The lake sat in a bowl of earth surrounded by mountains and pine trees on every side. Tahoe was the world's third clearest lake. Alexis had been waterskiing here before, and she remembered how she could see the bottom in places that were over one hundred feet deep. The lake was on the border of Nevada and California, with half of the lake in each state and the border running from north to south.

No matter which side of the lake you were on—the California side or the Nevada side—the lake was lined with plenty of resorts, vacation homes, and convention centers. In the winter, the area was also a popular place to ski and snowboard. Olympic medal winners had even been known to practice there.

Alexis had even seen these award winners practicing the last time she'd been at Lake Tahoe. Her dad attended conventions once or twice a year at the lake. And whenever they could, the whole Howell family accompanied him. They enjoyed the activities while Mr. Howell went to his business meetings.

Alexis recognized the landscape and held her breath for her favorite part of the drive. One last corner, and there it was. The view before them was a wonderful panorama. The brilliant lake shone in the sunlight like a perfectly smooth sapphire. The sight made Alexis gasp, even though she'd expected it. Suddenly the view was gone, replaced by walls and darkness.

Beep! Beep! Beep-Beep! Alexis's dad honked the horn.

"What's wrong?" Bailey jerked out of her slumber. "Are we falling off the cliff, Lexi?"

"Lexi? I'm Lexi now?" Alex asked with a smile. Bailey was well known for the nicknames she gave others.

Bailey didn't answer. She just grabbed Alexis's coat in fear. She frantically looked around. "It's dark!"

"No, Bailey! We're not falling off the cliff. We're passing through Cave Rock. It's a tunnel that has been around forever."

"Well, why was your dad honking the car horn?" asked Bailey, still a little dazed. "Scared me to death!"

"Sorry about that," said Alexis. "My dad honks

every time we go through a tunnel. This wasn't bad because the tunnel was short. You should have seen this one time! We were on the East Coast, and we went through this tunnel that was about a mile long. Dad honked *all the way through!* Doesn't your dad honk the car horn when you go through tunnels?"

"You really need to come to the center of the nation," Bailey answered. "Where I live, we're in the middle of the United States. The land is pretty flat there."

"Flat? You mean like the desert?"

"Well, we have hills and stuff. But we don't have mountains—especially not with tunnels," Bailey explained. "You have to go up to Wisconsin to see the bigger hills and huge rocks. They might have tunnels up there. I don't know."

Bailey lived near the middle of the state of Illinois, outside a city named Peoria. She was also still a preteen and the youngest of the group who called themselves the Camp Club Girls. The girls had all met when they shared a cabin at Lake Discovery Camp. They had become the best of friends as they solved a mystery together. And since then, the Camp Club Girls had continued to solve mysteries—mysteries that had baffled many adults!

As they drove into the resort area of Lake Tahoe,

Alexis pointed out the hotel and convention center where they'd be staying. "It's called a hotel, but it's really a resort," she said.

"What's the difference?" Bailey asked.

"I'm not sure," said Alex. "I think resorts have more activities going on, and this place has a ski run and all sorts of fun stuff.

"And we can also enjoy any of the activities in town. They have a great transportation system—it's a cute little shuttle bus that has places to get on and off it. So we can explore the whole city if we want," Alex explained.

In no time they had dropped off Mrs. Howell and the twins at the hotel. The girls waited in the car while Alexis's dad checked in Mrs. Howell and the boys and helped them get their luggage to the room. Then he returned to the van.

"Chauffeur's back," Mr. Howell announced cheerfully as he climbed into the driver's seat. "Next stop: Tahoe Animal Reserve."

Bailey and Alexis had their eyes wide open, trying to take in all the sights as Mr. Howell drove through town and out into land that was still on the brim of the lake, but not as filled with resorts.

In only moments they were pulling up a long, snowy

driveway to the animal reserve. A large wooden sign topped with snow read Tahoe Animal Reserve and Rescue. Mr. Howell parked in front of a small cabin that was painted a light shade of moss green. There was more than a foot of snow piled on the roof.

"I guess this is it!" said Mr. Howell. He got out of the car and immediately slid, nearly falling to the ground.

"Ouch!" he called. "Watch out for the ice!"

Just then the front door to the cabin opened, and a lady in a parka came running out.

"I'm so sorry!" she said. "I must have forgotten to put the salt out this morning!"

"Salt?" Bailey asked Alexis. She shut her door gently, trying to keep her footing. "Did I miss something?"

"Salt melts ice," said Alexis. "Something to do with lowering the freezing point of water."

"Very good!" said the woman. She reached down to help Alexis and Bailey up the steps. "You're a smart one! You must be the documentary girls."

"That's us!" said Bailey. "Are you ready to be famous? If we win, our video will be on the Discovery Channel!"

"That would be fabulous! I'm Karen Ingles. My husband and I own the reserve." Karen Ingles reached out to shake Mr. Howell's hand and then the girls' hands. "Come on in, you three! I'll show you around, and you can tell me more about your video."

The inside of the cabin was very cozy. Alexis noticed that it looked to be half house and half office. A roaring fire filled a beautiful stone fireplace. A few old couches were near the fire, and Alexis felt it would not just be a comfortable place to sit but would be a great location to film an interview or two. Looking toward the side of the cabin, Alexis could see a small kitchen and a large desk with papers strewed all over it. A door behind the desk led deeper into the cabin. Karen hung her parka on a coatrack and told the rest of them to do the same.

"Thank you so much for allowing us to do this, Mrs. Ingles," said Alexis.

"Please, Karen is fine. And don't mention it. We don't usually give tours, let alone allow people to film our animals, but your e-mail was so wonderful that I couldn't refuse. I could tell you two girls really cared about the animals, and it's a chance for college scholarships, too! Besides, you made me laugh."

Alexis smiled and was about to say something when her father yelped.

The girls spun around to see Mr. Howell jump up on the couch. He was shaking and pointing to something on the floor.

There, curled up on a rug in front of the fire, was a full-grown bobcat!

"Don't worry, sir," said Karen. "That's only Bubbles. He's kind of a pet."

Bubbles opened his eyes and lifted his nose in the air, sniffing.

"Dad, get off the couch!" said Alexis, embarrassed. "I don't think he's going to hurt you. Besides, you do know that bobcats can jump, right? The couch won't do you much good."

Everyone laughed. Mr. Howell even chuckled nervously as he stepped down off the striped cushion.

"Why do Bubbles's eyes look strange?" asked Bailey. She had crept closer and was sitting on the stone of the fireplace, only feet from the large cat.

"He's blind," said Karen. "That's the only reason he's kept as a pet. The vet couldn't fix his sight, so he'll never be released into the wild again. He'd die out there, so we let him stay here."

"That's so cool!" said Bailey. "I want a bobcat!"

"Well, some people do keep them as pets, but it's dangerous. They are wild, no matter how sweet and fluffy they look. See Bubbles's poufy paws? The claws in them are three inches long and could cut your throat in seconds."

Bailey backed slowly away and coughed.

"Oh, don't worry," said Karen. "He won't hurt you. We've had him for years. But that is something you need to remember while you're around the other animals in our sanctuary. No matter how cute they are, they're wild. They will react according to their instincts, no matter what your intentions are. Things like bats and raccoons can give you rabies, not to mention nasty scars. The owls' talons aren't very friendly either. If you're going to do this documentary, you have to remember to follow our rules, and never—*never*—approach any animal without us. Got it?"

"Yes, ma'am!" said Alexis. Bailey nodded her head so fast Alexis thought it might pop off. Alexis dug her little pink notebook out of her backpack. She wanted to write down the rules Karen gave her, as well as any information that might be great for the documentary.

Bang! Suddenly the door behind the desk burst open. A tall man in a flannel shirt stumbled into the room, his eyes bulging.

"Karen! The deal's off! Call those kids, and tell them that they can't film here! The mountain lions are out of their cages!"

Mischief and Mystery

It was obvious from the look on the man's face that he hadn't known the girls were there. He glanced around frantically.

"It's okay, Jake," said Karen. "Let's go get those cats back in their cages!" The two owners turned and ran out a back door.

"Wait!" said Alexis. "We can help!"

"What?" shouted Bailey, glancing at Bubbles nervously. "Didn't you hear? They said *mountain lions*!"

"I know! Come on!"

Before her father could stop her, Alexis followed Karen and Jake out the back door. Bailey was just behind. They followed a trail in the snow to a small barn structure not far away. Alexis reached out to open the door, but her father's large hand pushed it shut again.

"Dad!"

"Listen first, then open," said Mr. Howell. "The last

thing we want to do is let a sick mountain lion out of this barn."

Alexis was shocked. She thought for sure he was going to keep her from going in.

She and Bailey crept closer and put their ears against a small crack in the wood. They only heard the tramping of heavy boots and Jake's and Karen's panicked voices.

"Get that one! He's by your elbow!"

"No! Ow! The other one! She's too high up. You're going to have to get the ladder!"

But Alexis couldn't figure something out. She couldn't hear the mountain lions at all. Bailey seemed to be thinking the same thing.

"What? No ripping of claws? No earth-shattering roars?" she asked. Alexis shrugged and pushed the door open enough for the three of them to slide through. Just as she entered, something landed on her head and leaped ten feet to the top of one of the cages. It looked like a ball of fur with a tail.

There were six of them, and they were everywhere.

"They're kittens!" cried Bailey. "How cute! Come here, kitty, kitty. Come here."

Another ball of fluff tore by them, snagging Bailey's shoelace with a tiny, sharp claw.

"Oops. I forgot they had those things," said Bailey.

17

Alexis watched as Karen and Jake chased the litter of mountain lion cubs around and around the barn. They managed to get one back in the cage, but when they opened it again to put in another one, the first one escaped.

"It's useless!" cried Karen. "We'll be doing this all day!"

Another cub leaped from a rafter onto Alexis's head. This time it tried to stay put, but it was too heavy and slid to the floor instead.

"Ouch!" Alexis cried. "What's the deal?"

Bailey, who was reaching behind a barrel for one of the cubs, looked around.

"Lexi!" she cried. "It's your hat! The kittens like your hat!"

She was right! Alexis had forgotten about her hat. She had picked it out especially for this trip. It was a cozy striped winter hat with a huge fluff-ball pom-pom attached to a string at the top. Of course the lions would like it! The way the pom-pom bobbed, it looked like a huge cat toy!

Alexis studied the cage. She thought she could get the kittens in with her big pom-pom hat. If she walked in the cage, they would probably bound after her to get the fuzzy cap. But she couldn't figure out how she'd get out again without releasing them.

The cages in this barn were for larger animals. They were made of simple chain-link fencing—something Alexis could easily reach her arm through. Before anyone noticed, Alexis was climbing up the side of the mountain lion cage.

"What are you doing, Alexis?" asked her dad. He was following Jake around the barn trying to help. Instead, he ran into Jake every time he stopped, causing him to miss a kitten more than once.

"Don't worry, Dad! I think I have an idea!" Alexis reached the top of the cage and crawled carefully to one of the back corners. Then she took her hat off and shoved it through the chain link into the cage. She held it by the rim, allowing the huge fluff ball to dangle and swing.

"Here, kitty, kitty!" she called. It didn't work. The mountain lion cubs were way too interested in terrorizing the rest of the barn. "Bailey, help me! Get their attention!"

"Okay!" Bailey picked up a broom and ran over to the lion cage. She began running the handle along the metal, making a huge ruckus.

"Come on, kitties! Over here! Come on, kitties!"

The cats started noticing the noise and looked toward the dangling hat. Then, as if by some secret command, all six of them charged toward Bailey as fast as they could.

"*Ahhh!* Yikes!" Bailey screeched and lurched out of the way. "Lexi, it's working! Here they come!"

"Wait, Bailey!" said Alexis. "You have to open the door. They can't get in."

"Oh, right," said Bailey. She ran back over to the cage and struggled to open it against the tide of fluff and claws. Once it was cracked wide enough, the kittens pushed their way in. They dashed to the dangling hat and leaped, one after another, into the air. Their tiny paws reached over and over for Alexis's hat, but she pulled it out of reach every time.

"Are they all in?" Alexis called to Karen. Karen counted out loud.

"Yes! They are. Close the door!"

Bailey slammed the door, and Jake rushed to lock it before the kittens could run out again.

Alexis yanked her hat back through the cage and climbed carefully down. The ordeal was over with only one minor casualty: Alexis had lost one long piece of red yarn from her hat, and all six of the mountain lion cubs fought for it.

"Wow, that was great!" said Karen. "Thanks for your help, girls!"

Mr. Howell was still trying to detangle himself from a stack of buckets he had knocked over.

"Yeah," said Jake, pointing to Alexis's hat. "I guess I need to get one of those."

"Does this happen often?" asked Bailey.

"Well, it's not supposed to," said Karen.

"And it never used to," said Jake.

Alexis pushed her hat back onto her head and straightened it. "What do you mean, it never *used to?*" she asked.

"Come back to the office, and we'll tell you all about it," said Karen. She led the guests back through the snow and toward the cozy office.

"What's this?" Bailey asked. She stooped and dug something out of the snow. It was a small key ring with a few tiny golden keys on it.

"That's funny," Karen said. "I could have sworn those were in the office. Thanks!"

She took the keys and opened the office door.

"Looks like we need more firewood," said Jake, looking at the dying fire.

"I can help you get it," said Mr. Howell. Jake stepped right back out the door, looking scared.

"No, no, that's all right. Why don't you pour yourself some coffee over there?"

Mr. Howell fixed himself a cup of coffee. He brought the girls some hot cocoa, too, as well as a plate of doughnuts. Soon they were all circled around the living room fire. They could hear Jake splitting a few larger logs just outside.

"This has happened a lot lately," said Karen. She stirred some more sugar into her coffee and tasted it.

"What has?" Alexis asked. "The mountain lions getting out?"

"Well, yes and no. They *do* keep getting out, but other things are happening, too. Animals are getting loose when they shouldn't. But others have gotten sick or started acting strangely. One or two have escaped altogether, and that's a nightmare. In weather like this, there are very few animals that can survive. If they're not healthy or fully grown, they really don't stand a chance."

"So this is new?" Bailey asked, with her mouth full of doughnut. She swallowed, wiped frosting from her lips, and tried again. "I mean, it's never happened before?"

"No, not until recently," said Karen. "Jake's mom and dad owned this place long before we came along. It's been in the family forever, and nothing like this has ever happened. Jake feels like he's failing and is afraid we'll lose the family business. He just can't figure out what's going wrong."

Jake came back through the door and dropped a pile of wood in a box near the fireplace. Bubbles the bobcat jumped up and glared at Jake through his misty eyes before moving to the other side of the rug.

"So you see," Jake said, "it's like I said before we ran to the barn. You girls can't do your documentary here. It's just too dangerous. We never know when this stuff is going to happen. This time it was the cute little guys, but what if it's something bigger and more dangerous next time?"

Karen sighed. "That's why we don't give tours. If a visitor got hurt by a sick animal, that would be awful. We could get into a lot of trouble, not to mention the fact that we would feel horrible."

Alexis was heartbroken. They couldn't be serious, could they? She loved snowboarding, but she had really come here to do this documentary. Where else could she find a place like this reserve? This was the only one of its kind in all of California. And this was the only spring break she would get. She wouldn't have time to shoot the video after school started again next week.

"But we're not just anyone!" said Bailey. Alexis looked at her friend and smiled. She could tell that

Bailey would not take no for an answer. "I mean, we helped you catch the baby mountain lions, right? And no one got hurt. We're really smart, and we're always careful! We've done all kinds of things that other kids haven't, right, Lexi? Our club has solved all kinds of real mysteries, and if this isn't a mystery, then I don't know what is."

"What club is that?" Karen asked, sipping her coffee.

"The Camp Club Girls," Bailey explained. "We all met at Discovery Camp and solved a mystery there. Since then we've solved several mysteries together."

"Oh, so you all live in the Sacramento area?" Karen asked.

"No," Alexis said. "Only I live in California. The other girls live in different places in the United States—Montana; Washington, DC; Texas; Philadelphia—and Bailey here is from Peoria, Illinois."

Jake ran his thick hands through his hair and sighed.

"Sorry, kids. First of all, this isn't a mystery. It's just a case of too many mistakes made by *me*."

"That's not fair, Jake," said Karen. "We've been running things as usual. Name one mistake you have actually made."

Jake just stood, frowning.

"That's because you're not making mistakes," said

Karen. "Ever since this started, we've been even more careful!"

"But if it's not a mistake, Karen, what is it?"

"It's a mystery," said Mr. Howell. "It sounds like you *do* have a mystery on your hands."

Jake crossed his arms. "Prove it," he said jokingly.

"Okay," said Alexis, jumping to the challenge. "First of all, how did those cubs get out this morning? Who opened the cage last?"

"I did," said Karen. "This morning when I fed them, I opened it to check on Tiny Tim. He's the runt of the litter, and I had to make sure the others didn't take his share."

"Okay, so can you remember everything you did, step-by-step?" asked Bailey.

"Of course. I waited for Tiny Tim to finish eating, and then I left, locking the door behind me. Then I brought the keys inside and hung them on the rack. I remember I locked it because I had to try three keys before I found the right one. They all look the same."

"Little and gold?" asked Bailey. "Were they the keys I found outside in the snow?"

"As a matter of fact, they were," said Jake, puzzled. "I saw you put the keys on the rack this morning, Karen. How'd they get outside again?"

"You see?" said Alexis. "It's a mystery. You both know the keys got put away this morning, and you're sure the door was locked. The door was *open* when we went into the barn, which means *someone* must have taken the keys out of the office and opened the cage."

"But that's impossible!" said Jake. "We've been in here all morning!"

"No," said Karen.

"What?" Jake asked, puzzled.

"No we haven't. We both left to pick up Lisa from the bus stop this morning. We were gone for about fifteen minutes." She turned to the girls. "Lisa is our daughter. She's out right now, but you'll love her, I'm sure."

Jake and Karen stared at each other wide eyed. Could someone have broken into their beloved reserve and let these animals out on purpose?

"So you see, this *is* a mystery," said Bailey.

"And we can help you solve it while we do our documentary," said Alexis. "Maybe we'll catch something on tape that will help us figure out what's going on."

The girls looked sweetly up at the two reserve owners. Their big eyes pleaded for the chance to do their video and solve a mystery at the same time.

"Okay," said Jake. "But you won't be allowed to go anywhere on the reserve alone. One of us, or Lisa, will be with you at all times for your safety. If at any time things get too dangerous, we will pull the plug on the project. Sound fair to you?"

"Yes!" chimed both girls at once.

"And you're okay with this, Mr. Howell?" Karen asked.

"Yep," he said. "As long as they're supervised. Alexis almost got eaten by a T. rex last summer, so I'm sure she can handle some sick animals." Jake and Karen looked puzzled. Mr. Howell winked. "It's a good story. You should ask her about it sometime."

Threatening News

"I hope we can do all of this, Lexi," said Bailey.

She followed Alexis through the breakfast-buffet line, stopping every few feet to make sure she wasn't about to drop their camera bag. It was just a little too heavy for her. But Alexis didn't notice. She just kept piling cream cheese on her bagel.

"All of what?" she asked.

"I mean, I hope we can shoot this documentary *and* solve a mystery," Bailey said, the camera bag slipping off her shoulder. "We're only here for a few days, you know."

"It's almost a whole week," Alexis said, putting the top back onto her bagel. "Besides, we're the Camp Club Girls! Or have you forgotten? We can solve things like this in our sleep."

Bailey smiled and pushed the camera bag back on her shoulder. Then she dumped milk onto her bowl of fruity cereal.

"I guess you're right," she said. "Hey, there's a table

open by the fireplace!"

The girls gingerly stepped around the other tables and chairs in the room to a knobby wooden table in front of a huge stone hearth. The hotel they were staying in was amazing. It was massive, but it still felt warm and inviting.

Bailey set down her food tray and gasped.

"Oh no! Where's the camera?" She spun around to see if she had dropped it.

"Ouch!" someone behind her cried out.

Bailey turned and realized that she had hit the boy at the next table with the camera bag. It had been on her shoulder the whole time.

"I'm so sorry!" she said, turning to the boy. He looked a little bit younger than Alexis.

"Everyone's always sorry!" exclaimed the boy. "Why don't people try watching what they're doing and where they're going? Then they wouldn't have to be sorry all the time!"

"Um, well, we are really sorry," said Alexis. She was now standing beside Bailey looking down at the boy, who was still rubbing a spot on his head. "My friend was just worried. She thought she might have lost—"

"I really don't care what she thought she lost," the boy said, facing Alexis. "She just needs to watch where she's swinging her stuff."

He got up and stormed off, taking his tray to the other side of the dining room.

Alexis turned around and saw tears in Bailey's eyes.

"It's okay, small fry," Alexis said. "Some people can't help but spread their bad moods."

"I really didn't mean to hit him, Lexi," said Bailey. "I was thinking about the camera, and I didn't realize he was sitting so close to our table."

"Don't worry about it," said Alexis. "Let's eat. We have a bus to catch, remember?"

After breakfast Alexis and Bailey waited outside the hotel for the bus that would take them across town. They were supposed to get off at a little convenience store and ice cream parlor that was near the reserve. Then Lisa, Karen and Jake's daughter, would meet them and drive them the rest of the way. She was home for spring break, too—only she was taking a break from college.

On the bus ride over, Alexis and Bailey went through their recording equipment. They had a digital video camera and enough disks to record hours upon hours of footage. Alexis had also borrowed an external microphone from her drama teacher at school. It would help them pick up voices and sounds from farther away. This could really come in handy when they recorded animals from a distance.

When the girls got to their stop, Lisa was already waiting for them on the porch of the store.

"You must be the documentary girls," she said. She shook their hands. She was wearing thick skiing mittens. A hat that matched her mittens covered most of her long, brown French braid.

"That's us!" said Alexis. "This is Bailey, and I'm Alexis."

"It's good to meet you," said Lisa. She led them to a red jeep that was still running in the nearby parking lot. It was toasty when the girls climbed in. "So my parents told me about the kitties escaping yesterday and your help in getting them back in the cage. I hear you two think these things aren't just accidents, that something fishy is going on up at the reserve?"

Alexis was nervous. Would Lisa laugh at them? Did she think it was silly that two girls wanted to investigate what was going on at her parents' place? She was in college, after all. She was probably really smart.

"Yep!" Bailey answered before Alexis could get the right words together in her mind. "Something *very* fishy is going on up there. I mean, animals just don't unlock their cages by themselves, do they?"

"No," Lisa said, pulling away from the store parking

31

lot onto the main road. "I guess they don't."

"And your parents have run this reserve for years without problems, right?" Alexis asked. "So if they haven't changed the way they do things, then there is no logical reason for things to be falling apart."

Alexis couldn't quite bring herself to look at Lisa. She was sure the girl was about to laugh at them.

"I couldn't agree with you more," said Lisa.

"Really?" cried Alexis.

"Of course. I've been telling my mom for a while that something's not quite right. I hope you two can help. I would love to, but I've been away at school. And even if I were here, I wouldn't know where to start an investigation!"

"Well you're in luck!" said Bailey. "That's what we do!"

"My mom and dad told me about your success with solving mysteries," Lisa said as she turned the car around a corner. "I went on the Internet last night and read about how you solved the problems at that dinosaur park. I hear you've helped with other adventures, too."

"Yes, a bunch of them!" Bailey exclaimed. "We helped find a missing millionaire. Lexi helped rescue some sea lions. Our Camp Club Girls group of sleuths also solved a problem with sabotage in Wisconsin, a plot to harm the president in Maryland, a mystery with horses, and bad stuff going on at the London Bridge in Arizona. We even found lost jewels in Amarillo, at the Cadillac Ranch!"

"Hey, I've been there," Lisa said.

"All six of us Camp Club Girls always work together to figure out the mysteries," Bailey said.

Lisa drove up the driveway to the reserve, but she passed the small cabin where the girls had met Jake and Karen the day before. Instead, she kept driving around a few barns until she stopped at one of the smaller ones in the back.

"What's this building?" asked Alexis.

"This is the building where we start your documentary!" said Lisa. She jumped out of the jeep and trotted off through the snow. "C'mon! Follow me!"

Bailey grabbed the video equipment off the seat next to her and followed Alexis out of the car. The snow was knee deep, and Bailey had a hard time keeping up with the two taller and older girls.

"You want me to carry something else?" called Alexis.

"No thanks!" said Bailey. "I'm almost there!"

Lisa was waiting for them at the door to the barn. When they got close, she put her finger to her lips to signal them to be quiet. She opened the door and ushered Alexis and Bailey inside.

The room was dark, and the only noises were a small series of squeaks coming from the farthest corner of the barn. Lisa flipped a light switch, and a few lightbulbs flickered to life above their heads. The barn was warmer than Alexis had expected it to be.

There must be heaters in here, she thought.

Lisa peeled off her coat, and Alexis and Bailey did the same. After hanging them on pegs near the door, Alexis and Bailey walked quietly over to the corner where Lisa was. It was the same corner the squeaks were coming from.

"What are those things?" asked Bailey. "Baby mice?"

Tiny brown bodies huddled together in the bottom of the cage. The only body parts Alexis could really see in the pile of fluff were a bunch of round, pink ears. Maybe Bailey was right. They sure did look like mice.

"No, they're not mice." Lisa laughed. "They're baby bats."

"What?" whispered Alexis.

"That's so cool!" Bailey said.

"Yeah," said Lisa. "We've been taking care of these for a while now. Eventually, when it gets warmer and they get bigger, we'll be able to let them go. But right now they don't have any parents, so they don't have a way to get food."

Lisa opened the cage and took out one of the little creatures.

"Wait!" said Alexis. "Let me get out the camera!" She took the bag from Bailey's shoulder and pulled out the camera. It was fully charged and had a new disk in it already. "Ready, Bailey?"

"Ready!" Bailey said. They had decided that Alexis would run the camera and that Bailey would do most of the on-camera work. Alexis loved movies and usually did her own commentaries when filming. But she knew how much Bailey longed to be a star. She knew that giving the younger girl the turn in front of the camera would be a gift that would make Bailey happy. And since Bailey was younger, Alexis figured it would make her feel more confident and sure of herself around the other Camp Club Girls.

"This is a baby California Myotis bat," said Lisa. She brought the small animal closer to the camera and stretched out one of its wings. With the wings expanded, the bat was much bigger than Alexis had expected it to be.

"At first we fed them on milk," said Lisa. "We twisted the corners of small rags, dipped them in warm milk, and let the baby bats suck the milk out of the rags. Now they're big enough to eat bugs."

She placed the bat back in its cage and pulled a jar from a nearby shelf. Using a spoon, she scooped what looked like maggots out of the jar and sprinkled them into the bottom of the cage, which looked like it was covered with a fine mesh.

"The mesh allows their little claws to grab hold," said Lisa.

"So they can crawl to get the food, right?" Bailey asked.

"Yup! Look!"

Sure enough, the baby bats had detached themselves from their pile and were crawling toward the wiggling food. Alexis had never seen anything so gross and so cool at the same time. She taped the feeding. Then she put the camera on a tripod so it would tape while she and Bailey helped Lisa clean out the owl cages.

Baby great horned owls sat above them on branches, watching curiously. They were big, even for babies. Each one was about eighteen inches tall, and their fluffy baby feathers made them look even bigger.

"I don't know why on TV owls are always shown as spooky or around scary places," Alexis said. "They don't seem creepy at all."

"Probably because they're nocturnal animals. They

mainly hang out at night and sleep during the day. Night animals seem spooky to most people. Can you see where they got their name?" Lisa asked as she shoveled dirty straw into a bucket.

"The feathers on their heads, above their eyes," said Bailey. "They look like horns!"

The day flew by, and before they knew it, the girls were walking to the office for some lunch.

"Uh-oh," said Lisa as they approached the small building.

"What is it?" asked Alexis. Lisa pointed to a shiny black Mercedes-Benz.

"That always means trouble," she said. "Or at least it means that Dad's going to be in a bad mood."

Alexis tromped up the steps with the others and entered the office.

"I'll be right back. You wait here," Lisa said as she disappeared into the other room.

Like the day before, a fire was burning in the fireplace. But Bubbles was nowhere to be seen. Instead, someone strange was at the counter talking with Jake. It was an older man in an expensive coat. His gray hair was slicked back away from his round face, and he hadn't taken off his sunglasses, even though he was no longer outside.

"Come on, Jake," the man was saying. "This is the last time I'm coming out here."

"Good," Jake said with a smile. "Then this is the last time I'll have to tell you no."

The other man slapped his hand down on the desk. "Jake, you can't be serious!"

"You know exactly how serious I am, Bruce. I don't want your money."

"You'll wish you'd taken my money when they shut you down," said Bruce. He had spoken in a quiet voice. Alexis was glad she had good ears.

Jake's smile vanished, and he leaned across the desk toward Bruce. "Is that a threat?" he growled.

"No, Jake, no! Of course not!" Bruce laughed, but Alexis thought it sounded fake—like he was trying too hard to make the right sound come out. "I just mean that you're in trouble. It seems like you've been having a few. . .*problems* here at the reserve."

"How would you know about that?" asked Jake.

"Oh please, Jake! This is Tahoe! Tourists or no tourists, it's a small town. People talk." Bruce took his car keys out of his pocket.

"You know where to find me if you change your mind, Jake," he said. He placed a card on the desk, and then he was gone. As Alexis moved closer, she saw that the card said *Bruce Benton, Land Developer.*

Jake picked up the card. "We can just throw that in the trash," he said as he tossed it into the wastepaper basket.

Karen and Lisa came through the door, each carrying a stack of mail.

"I saw that Benton guy's car and heard you talking to him. What was that all about?" Karen asked Jake as the ladies handed their piles of mail to him.

"Oh, same old stuff," he answered. He took some of the mail from her and started opening it. "Bill, bill, bill," he said. Then he stopped. "Another threat letter," he said. He tossed it onto the desk.

Alexis and Bailey had wandered over to look out the window, but now they hurried back to the desk.

"Really?" Alexis said. "You got a threat letter?"

On the desk was a sheet of white paper with different sizes of lettering on it. Someone had cut words out of a magazine and pasted them together.

You think you're helping, but you're interfering with nature. Leave the forest alone! It will heal itself! If you don't, more than letters will come your way!

No one had signed it.

"What in the world?" Alexis said. "This is awful!"

"It's not as bad as you think," said Lisa. "We actually get them a lot. A lot of people are unhappy with places like this reserve."

Bailey and Alexis looked at Jake. They were puzzled. How could anyone be angry with a place that helped animals?

"It's the same old thing, Alexis," said Jake. "You can't please everyone. Some people think we do too much." He pointed to the letter Alexis held in her hand. "Others think we don't do enough. Nothing ever comes of the letter, though. We don't worry about them. We keep them all, just in case something worse happens, but that's it."

Alexis was still alarmed. She had received a threatening note once before, and she remembered how scared she had been. It had made her feel like someone could jump out at her at any moment. She opened her mouth to mention it.

"*Ahhh!*" Karen suddenly cried out.

"Oh no, Jake! Look!" She was holding another open letter.

"Is it another threat?" asked Bailey.

Jake took the letter and looked it over.

"No," he said. "It's worse. It's a letter from the government. They say they've had complaints about our facility, and that if they continue, then we'll lose our license to operate."

"What does that mean?" asked Alexis. Lisa walked up and put her arm around her dad's waist.

"What it means, Alexis, is that we'll have to close down the reserve."

CHAPTER 4

Moneybags Bruce

I think there's a lot more going on in this mystery than I ever imagined.

Alexis typed the last line onto the screen for the Camp Club Girls to read. She was using her mom's laptop and had just typed a long e-mail to all the girls to let them know what was going on.

Bailey read over Alexis's shoulder.

"It's scary to think that not only is someone letting animals out of their cages but that the government has even heard about it," Bailey said thoughtfully.

"Well, as you read in my e-mail, I told the Camp Club Girls that if we can't solve this mystery, the reserve might not exist anymore. And that would be terrible!" Alexis exclaimed. "Then what would happen to those precious baby bats?"

"And animals that can't take care of themselves, like Bubbles," Bailey added.

"Good thing Mom and Dad picked this time to bring us here," Alex said.

"Or as Beth would say, 'There's no such thing as coincidence. God has you there now for a reason!'" Bailey laughed as she thought of their friend from Amarillo, Texas. Elizabeth was a walking Bible—and not because she was showing off, but because she believed that God directed people through His words in the Bible. Elizabeth believed God could do anything and often reminded the girls of that truth.

"I'm just concerned," Alexis said.

"About the mystery?" Bailey asked.

"Yes, but I'm also kind of worried that we won't be able to solve the mystery and do the documentary, too," she said slowly. "I really, *really* wanted to win this documentary contest, but what good will that be if the reserve we film gets shut down?"

Alexis bent over to lace up her heavy snowboarding boots.

Bailey had a mouthful of ski mittens as she used her hands to lace up her boots, but she nodded to show that she was listening.

"Karen and Jake are really doing us a favor by letting us film our video here," continued Alexis. "It would be sad if we couldn't pay them back by solving this case. I mean, it's what we *do*."

"So we'll just have to keep doing what we're doing," said Bailey, taking her gloves out of her mouth and tossing them onto the bed. "I mean, we'll solve the case *while* we work on the documentary."

"That's what I thought, too," said Alexis, "but that's a lot to do in a few days."

"No, Lexi!" said Bailey. "I mean *really* work on them at the same time. We were going to shoot a documentary about the reserve, right? Like, about what they do for the animals and stuff? But now something better has come up! They do amazing things for the wildlife here, and someone is paying them back by sabotaging them! So, we can still make our film about the reserve. . ."

A lightbulb flashed to life in Alexis's head.

"But we can make it about the *mystery*! Then filming our documentary really *is* solving the case! Bailey, you're a genius!"

Alexis hugged Bailey so hard that the two of them practically fell off the bed. The worry lifted like it had never been there.

Why didn't I think of that in the first place? Alexis wondered. *We can document the trouble at the reserve!*

If they solved the case, their documentary would

be different from any other—like a real-life *CSI* show!
And even if they didn't solve the case completely, they
would draw attention to what was happening. They
could send a copy to the government and maybe get
more help for Karen and Jake. *And I bet the Tahoe
Tourism Bureau would help, too,* Alexis thought.

The girls spent the morning on the ski slopes.
Alexis had promised her dad that she and Bailey would
take at least one day to enjoy the snow with the family.
It was a vacation, after all.

Alexis loved snowboarding. She had learned to
ski in fifth grade but had always felt awkward. In the
back of her mind, she was always afraid her legs would
tangle up at any moment and send her flying down the
mountain on her face.

The next year, her dad had signed her up for
snowboarding lessons. It was so much easier! Or at
least she thought so. There was no chance that her feet
could tangle, since they were anchored securely side by
side.

There had been one time that a face-plant had
brought the snowboard up from behind to whack her
in the back of the head. . .not fun. But overall it was
always a great time.

Bailey hadn't skied much, so the girls spent the

first hour on the bunny hill. Alexis taught her how to wedge the tips of her skis together (in the shape of a triangle), and they cruised along slowly until Bailey got the hang of it. It didn't take long. Soon she was tearing down the mountain so fast that Alexis could hardly catch up.

"You should have your camera along!" Bailey called to Alexis. "Then you could do a documentary on a midwestern girl learning to ski! I could be a star!"

On their fifth run down the mountain, Alexis took her time. She always got more confident after a few hours on the slopes, so she wanted to try some smaller jumps. By the time she got to the bottom, Bailey had been waiting for almost ten minutes.

"Come on, Lexi! You take forever!"

"Sorry! I wanted to try some tricks!"

"Well, I'm starving," said Bailey. "Let's get lunch!"

The girls left their boards outside the lodge and went in to find the cafeteria. They ordered a pizza to share and then giant cups of hot chocolate. Alexis had to admit that it felt good to take her gloves off and wrap her fingers around something warm.

"The sun's out," said Alexis. "Want to sit outside?"

"Sure," said Bailey. They wiggled their way through tons of tourists. Alexis thought she heard at least four different languages being spoken in the crowd. People came to Tahoe from all over the world it seemed. Alexis was trying to understand a woman speaking French when Bailey elbowed her in the ribs.

"Hey, look!" Bailey said. "Isn't that the boy I hit in the head with our camera at breakfast yesterday?"

Alexis looked in the direction Bailey was pointing. Sure enough, the same boy was sitting on a bench looking up at the mountain. Alexis wondered why he wasn't wearing any snow gear. Who came to the ski lodge and didn't ski? As the girls got closer, Alexis noticed something else. The boy was holding a walking stick. But it wasn't like the walking sticks people used when they hiked in the mountains. It was thinner and white.

"Bailey," Alexis whispered. "I think he's blind!"

"No way!" said Bailey. "Yesterday he walked all the way across the dining room without help. And he was carrying a tray of food!"

"I know, but that's normal. Blind people don't need help all the time—only when they're in unfamiliar or crowded surroundings. Come on."

And before Bailey knew what she was doing, Alexis was sitting down beside the boy on the bench. Bailey sat next to her, more than a little nervous. Was the boy still angry with her?

"Hi," said Alexis. "I'm Alexis, and this is my friend Bailey."

"Hi," squeaked Bailey. The boy didn't even turn to look at them when he spoke.

"Oh, it's you," he said. "Going to knock me in the head with a ski pole this time?"

"Of course not," said Alexis. She was trying to be friendly. The last thing she wanted to do was argue. "So what are you doing up here?" she asked.

"Observing," said the boy.

"Observing?" said Bailey. "But you're—"

"Blind? Yeah, thanks for reminding me. I almost forgot."

"We're sorry," said Alexis. "My friend was just curious. What kinds of things do you observe up here?"

The boy turned to Alexis but didn't say anything. Alexis got the feeling that he wanted them to leave.

"Are you on vacation?" asked Bailey.

"Yep. My family and I come every year."

"Do you ski or snowboard?" asked Alexis. Bailey was about to ask how he could do either, but Alexis shushed her.

"I would like to ski, but it's not going to happen this year. My dad is here in meetings on business so it's just my mom and me having free time. She forgot to reserve me a guide, and I'm not good enough to go down the mountain without one."

"Where is she?" asked Bailey. "Couldn't she guide you?"

"Nope. She never bothered to learn how." The bitterness in the boy's voice made Alexis sad. "Dad usually does it."

"So you're just going to sit around your whole vacation?" asked Bailey.

"Bailey!" said Alexis.

"No, she's right," said the boy. "That's about all I can do."

He leaned back on the bench and crossed his arms. Just then, Alexis had an idea.

"Hey!" she said. "We're filming a documentary at an animal reserve outside of town. We're taking today off, but we're going back tomorrow if you'd like to come!"

The boy's eyes looked less grumpy for a split second. Alexis could tell he was interested, even if he was pretending not to be.

"Come on," she said. "It will be fun."

"Okay," he said. "Sure. I mean, it's not like I have anything else to do. My name's Angelo."

"All right, Angelo," said Alexis. "Meet us in the

hotel lobby at seven thirty tomorrow morning. We take the bus across town. Your mom can call my mom if she has any questions." Alexis jotted her phone number on her receipt from lunch and thrust it into his hand.

Angelo nodded and then got up and walked away. Alexis noticed that he used his walking stick to find his way through the crowd.

"I think I made him mad again!" said Bailey.

"I'm sure you didn't," said Alexis. "You were just curious. I'm sure he knows you're not rude. People probably get their words all mixed up around him all the time. Plus, he's coming with us tomorrow. You can show him how awesome and sweet you really are!"

"Okay," said Bailey. "But Lexi, I think we have a new mission now."

"What?" said Alexis. "Another one?"

"Yep. Whatever it takes, we're going to make Angelo smile."

The girls walked back through the lodge. There were still a few hours of daylight left, and they could get at least five runs in if they hurried. Near the front door, Alexis stopped. Bailey ran into her from behind.

"Ouch! What'd you stop for?"

"Look over there," said Alexis. "That man by the

fireplace—isn't he the man who was at the reserve yesterday? Jake called him Bruce."

Sure enough, there he was, warming his hands by the fire and talking to the owner of the ski resort. Alexis didn't know why, but she just *had* to hear what they were saying.

"Let's sit by the fire for a minute," she said. "There are two chairs open."

So Alexis and Bailey sat next to the fire in a pair of squishy armchairs and strained to hear every word they could.

"How's the new resort coming, Bruce?" asked the second man.

"Too slow for my taste," answered Bruce. "I'm having some trouble getting the land I want."

"The city isn't giving you trouble, is it?"

"No, no," said Bruce. "It's the owners. They're not interested in selling, no matter how much I offer! I don't get it. The money I could give them would buy five animal reserves somewhere else! What's so special about this one?"

"You're trying to buy from Jake and Karen?" asked the other man. "I don't think you'll win that battle. That reserve is Jake's whole life."

"That's what he said, too. But I wouldn't be so sure.

Money always gets people in the end, and I always get what I want."

The two men walked off toward the cafeteria. Alexis turned to look at Bailey, whose mouth was hanging open.

"That's why he was at the reserve yesterday!" said Bailey. "Moneybags Bruce wants to buy it!"

"Yeah," said Alexis. "And it sounds like he'd do anything to get it, too."

"I'm going to write down the clues we're looking at right now," Alexis added.

She unzipped a pocket in her snowboarding pants and took out her small pink notebook. It was time to start taking notes on this case. Alexis had gotten in the habit of carrying a small notebook with her everywhere she went. She'd seen it done on one detective show on TV and thought it was a good idea. And her notebook had come in handy before as she'd worked on other Camp Club Girl mysteries.

"We already know someone probably unlocked the mountain lion cage," said Alexis as she scribbled. "You found the keys in the snow, and Karen swore they had been hanging up inside that morning. Then we have that threat letter, too. Maybe we can take a closer look at it tomorrow."

Last but not least, Alexis wrote the most recent piece of information:

"Moneybags" Bruce Benton wants to buy the reserve to put up another ski resort. Would he sabotage the reserve to get what he wants? He did say he would do anything. . . .

"Come on," Bailey said. "Let's go to our room. We need to send an e-mail to the Camp Club Girls to fill them in! They need to know about the mountain lions and Moneybags Benton saying he'd do anything to get the reserve."

CHAPTER 5

Bellyaches and Bears

The bus ride the next morning was pretty quiet. Alexis and Bailey tried over and over to get Angelo to talk to them, but he only nodded his head or shrugged his shoulders. By the time they got to the reserve, Alexis was sure that since Angelo was with them, it would be a very long day.

"Things have been a little crazy here," said Lisa as she led them into the office.

"What do you mean?" asked Bailey. But as soon as they saw Karen, they knew something was up. She was sitting at the desk, staring blankly at a cup of coffee that looked as if it had gone cold. Large dark circles were under her eyes.

"Been up all night?" asked Alexis. Karen jerked out of her stupor and nodded.

"The coyotes are sick. I was up late taking care of them. Then, when I finally went to bed, the phone rang. It was three in the morning."

"Who in the world would call you at three in the morning?" asked Bailey.

"That's what we're trying to figure out," said Karen. "I answered, thinking it might be an emergency, but I only heard breathing. Then a voice said, 'You're lucky they're only sick this time.' And the phone went dead."

"It was a threat?" asked Angelo. It was the first time he'd spoken.

"Yes," said Karen. "I guess it was. Alexis, who's your friend?"

"This is Angelo. We met him at our hotel, and he was interested in our documentary. I hope it's okay that we brought him along."

"That's fine," said Karen. She walked over to where Angelo was standing and grabbed his hand to shake it. "It's nice to meet you, Angelo. You all want some hot chocolate?"

Alexis took out her pink notebook while the group sat down on the squishy couches near the fireplace. She hadn't expected to have new information so quickly, but now seemed like the perfect time to ask some questions. Karen set five cups of cocoa on the coffee table and sat down.

"Karen, you said the call came at three in the morning, right?" asked Alexis. "Do you remember what the voice sounded like?"

"Well, it was definitely a man's voice. I didn't recognize it, so it wasn't anyone I know. It was kind of high pitched."

Alexis scribbled down every word. Bailey took a gulp of her cocoa then put it down.

"What if the caller was just disguising his voice?" she asked. "Like this?"

Bailey said the last two words in a silly high-pitched voice that reminded Alexis of Elmo. She laughed.

"That's possible," said Karen. "I was also exhausted. I mean, it *was* three in the morning. Jake probably could have called, and I wouldn't have recognized him."

That made everyone laugh, including Angelo. Bailey elbowed Alexis and pointed. It really was nice to see him smile.

"Someone's at the back door," said Angelo suddenly. Everyone turned, and sure enough Jake opened the door, stomping snow off his boots. Bailey leaned over to Alexis and whispered in her ear.

"How did he know there was a back door?" she asked. Alexis had been wondering the same thing. But Lisa answered.

"I imagine he has amazing ears," she said. Angelo grinned.

"That's what my dad says," he said. "It's fun to freak people out sometimes though."

"Often when people don't have their sight or hearing, their other senses become keener to help their bodies and minds compensate," Lisa explained. "Often, blind people can hear better than the rest of us. Or they may be able to distinguish odors that the rest of us can't even smell."

"Looks like you guys are having a party," said Jake. He leaned over the back of the couch and spoke to Karen. "The coyotes are getting worse, and the vet can't come till tomorrow."

"Okay, I'll be right out," Karen said.

"Can we come?" asked Alexis. "We don't have to film the sick animals, but we could look for clues. I mean, I really think whoever called you did this on purpose. Didn't they say something about the sick animals?"

"They sure did," said Jake. "We just don't know *how* they made them sick. Did they poison them, or what? We can't help the coyotes until we know what's making them sick. But I don't know if you should go near them. . . ."

He looked around at the concerned group and sighed.

"Okay," he said after a minute of silence. "Come on

out. And grab the cameras. There might be some stuff worth filming."

Lisa left to do some other chores, but everyone else followed Jake to the coyote barn. Angelo didn't have his walking stick, but apparently he didn't need it. He followed close beside Bailey with his hand on her elbow and never stumbled.

"Just let me know if we have to go up or down stairs," he said, tapping Bailey gently on the head.

"You got it!" she said. She was glad he didn't seem to be angry with her anymore.

The coyotes were a very sad sight. They were all curled up in their cages, whimpering, and one or two of them were barely breathing. Alexis felt a surge of anger. Who could do this to poor defenseless animals in cages? And *why?*

She noticed that most of the coyotes had bandages or casts on. So they had already been hurt before someone came in and made them very ill.

"Someone is definitely not playing fair," said Alexis. She took out her camera and began shooting footage of the poor creatures.

"Bailey," she whispered, "get on camera and explain what's happening."

Bailey smoothed out her short hair and jumped in

front of the camera next to the first coyote cage.

"Today, we came to the reserve excited to help, but the day has turned sad. Someone broke in during the night and gave the coyotes something to make them ill. Since we have no way to know what they have eaten, it's hard for Karen to treat them. Everything will have to go on hold until Karen, Jake, and Lisa can figure out how to help these poor creatures."

"And cut!" said Alexis. "Good job, Bailey. That was great."

Alexis was stuffing the camera back in the bag when Angelo grabbed Bailey by the arm.

"Don't move," he said. "What did you just step on?"

Bailey looked down at her boots.

"Nothing, unless you count the straw on the floor," she said.

"No," said Angelo. "It was definitely *not* straw."

Angelo knelt down and tapped Bailey's left boot. "Lift this one up, please. If you could."

Bailey looked puzzled, but she did what Angelo asked. She lifted her boot, and he placed his hand on the floor. He moved the straw around for a minute and shook his head.

"Nope. Can you lift the other one?" Bailey did what he said, and Angelo searched the straw again. After a few seconds, he lifted his arm up in triumph.

"Here it is!" he said. "What is it? It feels like foil."

"It *is* foil," said Alexis. "It's a chocolate wrapper!"

"A what?" asked Jake. He came across the barn and looked at the crumpled piece of brown foil.

"A chocolate wrapper," said Alexis again. "You guys don't eat in here, do you?"

"Of course not," said Jake. "Karen! Good news! It's just chocolate!"

Karen came over to look at the wrapper as well.

"This is good news?" asked Bailey. "Maybe they just ate too much! I get sick every Easter because I eat too many chocolate eggs. I guess it wouldn't be so bad if I didn't combine them with jelly beans."

"Well, chocolate isn't *good* for them, but at least now we know what to do for them," said Jake.

"So is it like the time my cousin's dog ate my giant candy bar?" Alexis asked. "We thought the puppy was going to die."

"Yes, something like that," Jake said. "Chocolate can kill dogs in the worst cases, and coyotes are of the dog family, so chocolate can make them very sick, too."

"Wow, Angelo," said Alexis. "We wouldn't have found that wrapper if you hadn't been with us. I'm really glad you came!" Angelo smiled. Again. Alexis was really glad he had decided to come with them. Not just because he found the wrapper, but because she was sure this was taking his mind off the fact that he couldn't ski. She tucked the wrapper into her notebook to keep as evidence.

This keeps getting weirder and weirder, she thought. Someone had wanted to make the coyotes ill but hadn't gone far enough to kill them. Maybe the person had a soft spot after all. Or maybe he or she was too afraid to poison the coyotes with something more toxic, like antifreeze.

Not only did someone feed the coyotes chocolate, but then they had called Karen in the middle of the night. What was it the caller had said? *You're lucky they're only sick this time.*

Does that mean that next time they will *kill an animal?* Alexis was suddenly afraid for all the animals on the reserve. Why would someone do something like this? What could they have to gain?

God, Alexis prayed, *please help us get to the bottom of this before one of your creatures gets hurt.*

Her thoughts were interrupted by Lisa, who came into the barn carrying an armload of helmets.

"You three want to take a ride?" she asked. "I thought I could show you the bear caves today!"

Alexis looked at Bailey and smiled.

"Awesome!" said Bailey. "Do the bears go away in the winter?"

"Of course not!" said Lisa. "But they do hibernate. They're all sleeping right now."

Bailey's smile wavered, but she was the first one to run outside and climb onto the monstrous snowmobile that Lisa indicated. It was big enough for all four of them. Lisa climbed onto the front, so she could drive, and Bailey held on to her coat. Alexis and Angelo climbed up behind Bailey.

"Hold on tight!" Alexis said to Angelo over her shoulder.

"You, too!" he said. "It won't do me any good to hold on to you if you fall off!"

The ride up the mountain was fun. Alexis had never ridden on a snowmobile before. Most of the wind was blocked by Bailey's hat, but her nose was still starting to tingle in the cold. It felt strange—almost like they were sledding uphill.

When Lisa stopped the vehicle, Alexis was confused. She couldn't see a cave anywhere.

"We have to walk the rest of the way," Lisa explained. "We can't take the snowmobile any closer because it's too loud. The last thing we want to do is wake a hibernating bear!"

Lisa went to the back of the snowmobile and untied a big bundle. She pulled out four pairs of snowshoes. Alexis strapped on the purple ones. She was really excited. She had heard of snowshoes but had never worn them herself. They really did allow her to walk on *top* of the deep snow!

Alexis took the camera out of its bag and began taping. She felt like she was in a scene from *The Call of the Wild.* It was one of her favorite books.

The group hiked for about five minutes before Lisa stopped them.

"There, up ahead," she said. "Can you see it?"

Alexis had to strain her eyes, but she could just see the cave. It was a small, black opening in the snow beneath a huge pile of granite. The pine trees were heavy with snow. They bent in toward the cave, as if they were protecting it from outsiders.

"We won't get too much closer," said Lisa. "Just to be safe. But I thought you might like to get it on tape."

Alexis moved a few feet to the left to get a better angle. Angelo was still barely holding on to her back.

"Can you smell them?" he asked.

"Who? The bears?" asked Bailey.

"Of course. I wouldn't want to get too close. Never

mind the teeth and claws. They stink!"

Alexis couldn't smell a thing. She zoomed in with the camera lens, and Bailey said a few words into the camera. Alexis was about to turn around when Angelo's grip on her coat tightened.

"What is it?" she asked him.

"A sound," he said. "I heard a strange sound. . .one that doesn't belong in this forest."

"What kind of sound?" asked Alexis, but then she heard it—a small popping noise—right before something hard stung her cheek.

"Ow!"

Alexis stumbled and almost pulled Angelo onto the ground. There were a few more popping noises, and then a completely different sound tore through the forest.

It was the roar of a cranky bear.

"Run!" called Lisa. She grabbed Bailey and took off toward the snowmobile. Alexis and Angelo followed, but the snowshoes were hard to run in. Alexis looked back just in time to see a huge brown bear emerge from the mouth of the cave. It took one sleepy look around and started running right for them!

Fortunately the snowmobile was a bit downhill from the bear cave. That downhill slope helped the young humans run faster, while it slowed down the bear. Alexis briefly remembered a Discovery Channel special on bears, which revealed that bears run uphill much faster than they run downhill.

Of course it's not good to have bears running after you, fast or *slow!* she thought.

Lisa and Bailey reached the snowmobile and clambered on. Lisa fired up the engine and turned to pull Alexis and Angelo aboard. Soon they were on their way back down the mountain. Alexis turned to see if the bear was still following them, but she wasn't holding on to Bailey. She slipped sideways and fell into the snow. She hit hard and rolled down the mountain about ten feet before stopping near a half-buried tree stump.

Lisa circled back around, and Angelo helped pull Alexis back onto the snowmobile.

"Good thing I wasn't holding on to you!" he laughed.

"Wait!" said Alexis. "My camera! I dropped it when I fell!"

Luckily the bear had taken off in another direction, and the camera was easy to find. It was right where Alexis had fallen, tangled up in a pile of dead branches. The branches kept it from falling into the wet snow, which might have damaged it.

"It's still on," said Bailey. "You might not want to waste the battery!"

The group headed back to the office. All of them were quiet. They knew that they had barely escaped being attacked by an angry bear. What were those strange noises? And what could have awakened the bear? Alexis asked Jake her questions back at the office, but he wasn't worried about answering them at the moment.

"The most important thing, Alexis, is that we find that bear! We need the tranquilizer gun, Karen. Call the ranger, too. Maybe if we put it back in its den, it will sleep out the rest of the winter."

"What if you can't find it?" asked Bailey.

"That's what we're worried about," said Karen. "Bears that wake up early run into lots of problems. Right now, most of the smaller animals are hibernating, too, and the rivers are frozen over. There isn't much food out there for a bear. If he's awake long, he'll burn up all of the fat he stored for the winter, and then he'll have to be put in captivity or. . ."

"Or what?" asked Alexis.

"Or he'll die," said Jake.

Kate's Helping Hand

Back at the hotel, the girls left Angelo to go meet
Alexis's family for dinner. First they went to the room
to change clothes. When Alexis looked in the mirror,
she saw a huge red bruise with a purple center on her
right cheek.

"Eew!" she said. "That looks awful! Bailey, why
didn't you say anything?"

"Well, we were too worried about the bear, weren't
we?" said Bailey. "Besides, it didn't look that bad at the
reserve. It's definitely pretty."

Alexis pressed her fingers gently to her cheek.

"Ouch! What could have done this?" she asked. "I
remember getting hit with something before the bear
woke up, but I never saw what it was."

"Could it have been a rock?" asked Bailey.

"Maybe. Oh well. We'd better get down to the
restaurant."

Alexis threw on fresh jeans and a sweater before

slipping on her sneakers. They were so much easier to walk in than her heavy snow boots. After tromping in boots all day, she felt as light as a feather. Bailey tied her hair up in a tiny ponytail, and they took the elevator to the second floor to find the steak house.

"There they are!" said Bailey, pointing into the crowded restaurant. Alexis looked up and saw her two brothers waving their arms to get her attention. Her mother was frantically grabbing water glasses to keep them from being knocked over.

Alexis sat down next to her father, and he poked gently at her cheek.

"I thought you two were shooting a documentary out there, not BB guns!" he said.

"BB guns?" said Alexis.

"Yeah," said Mr. Howell. "I'd recognize a BB bruise anywhere! My brother and I used to play with those things all the time. It's a miracle we never shot an eye out."

Alexis's eyes opened wide, and she kicked Bailey under the table. So she had been shot by a BB gun? That meant someone else had been out at the bear cave at the same time as their group. What if a BB had awakened the bear? What if that's what the person was trying to do?

It reminded Alexis of Cruella DeVille, the villain in *One Hundred and One Dalmatians.* Her first name started with the word *cruel*, and in the movie she would have done anything to get the puppies for a fur coat. If turning cute puppies into a coat wasn't cruel, Alexis didn't know what was.

She thought about how it felt to see the bear charge out of the cave. It had been really scary. One of them could have gotten hurt, or even worse. At that moment, Alexis knew she and Bailey and the Camp Club Girls had to solve this case as soon as possible. The person doing these things was becoming dangerous. Like Cruella's character, they didn't care who they hurt. As long as they got what they wanted, they might do anything. . .but what *did* they want?

After dinner Alexis and Bailey took their camera to their hotel room and borrowed Mrs. Howell's computer again. Alexis plugged her camera into the USB port on the computer so the girls could look at what they'd filmed near the bear cave. The camera had been rolling the entire time. Maybe it saw something— or *someone*—that they hadn't.

They started by watching the spot on the sick coyotes.

"You do such a great job in front of the camera, Bailey!" said Alexis.

"Thank you, dah-ling," said Bailey. She tossed her hair and did her best movie-star impression.

"We have to remember to add the stuff about the chocolate," said Alexis. "I don't think we filmed—"

"Shhh!" said Bailey. "Here's the bear cave!"

They sat and watched as the camera rolled over the snowy landscape. Surrounding pine trees were drooping from the weight of the snow. Shafts of sunlight peeked through the branches and made the white sparkle. Soon the cave came into view—a small opening beneath the rock.

"Is it just me, or does that cave look too small for a bear to get in and out of?" asked Bailey.

"Well, a bear sure did come out of it," said Alexis. "We're about to see it happen."

The camera rocked a little.

"That must have been when you got hit by the BB," said Bailey.

Alexis nodded. She was watching the screen as closely as possible. Soon the bear came charging out of the cave, throwing snow everywhere. But Alexis wasn't watching the bear. She was looking everywhere else for any sign of a fifth person in that forest.

Soon the film got hard to watch. The picture jumped all over the place as Alexis tried to run in her snowshoes. Most of the shots showed either her clumsy feet or a piece of the sky.

"Well, that's it," said Bailey. "That's where you dropped the camera when you fell off the snowmobile, right?"

"Yup," said Alexis. "Now all we can see is snow and a couple trees." Alexis reached for the Eject button, but Bailey grabbed her hand.

"Wait! I see something," she said. "Rewind it!"

Alexis skipped back a few frames and leaned in closer. Sure enough, something was moving in the background. Near a group of trees in the distance, a shadowy figure climbed onto something and sped away in the opposite direction.

"Was that another snowmobile?" asked Bailey.

"I believe it was," said Alexis. "What else could it have been? Bailey! We have this person on tape! Whoever was out there waking up the bears—"

"*And* shooting people with BB guns," said Bailey.

"Right. That, too. They're on our video, Bailey! This is great! All we have to do is blow up this frame, and we'll have a picture. What if this solves the case?"

"That would be great," said Bailey. "Can we blow up the picture on this computer?"

Alexis messed around with the keyboard for a few minutes and then sighed. There were hardly any programs loaded onto it.

"No, we can't," said Alexis. "I mean, there might be a way, but I have no clue how to do it without the program I'm used to using at school. I wish Kate were here. She would know how to do it."

Bailey laughed so loud that someone talking outside their hotel room abruptly stopped.

"Come on, Lexi! Do you or do you not know how to e-mail?"

Alexis couldn't help it. She began laughing, too. Why had she forgotten all about the Internet? It was her main link to the rest of the Camp Club Girls.

"Right," Alexis said, going to work at the keyboard again. "All I need to do is cut out this piece of video and send it to Kate. I hope the file won't be too big."

After a few minutes of tweaking the video file, Alexis typed an e-mail to send to their friend, the technogeek, and copied in the rest of the Camp Club Girls so they'd know what was going on. If anyone could help them, Kate could.

Dear Kate,

Bailey and I were going to see sleeping bears today when someone woke them up! Apparently the person shot a BB gun into their den (and hit

*me with one, too!). I have a video with a person
in the background. The person is too far away to
see now, but I was hoping you would know how
to zoom in and maybe get a few still pictures. I
hope this isn't asking too much. As Princess Leia
said in the old* Star Wars *movie: "You're our only
hope!"*

*This could be the big break we need. Bailey
says, "Hi, Katie Cat!" We love you and miss you!*
Alex and Bailey

"Hopefully she'll get to it soon," said Bailey.

"Are you kidding? Kate checks her e-mail every five
minutes. If she's not already asleep, she'll probably get
it tonight."

Just then there was a gentle knock at the con-
necting door, and Mrs. Howell popped her head in.

"Hi, Mom. We're done with the computer now,"
Alex announced.

"Oh, that's okay. I didn't come in for that," Mrs.
Howell explained. "I got a call from the restaurant.
They said I left my purse there, and they've taken it to
the front desk. I'm trying to get your brothers to bed,
so I wondered if you girls would run down and get it
for me."

"Sure, Mom," Alex said with a smile.

"Great. I'll call them and let them know you're on the way," Mrs. Howell said.

The girls quickly entered the elevator and rode to the lobby.

"I wonder how Angelo's doing," Bailey said.

"Hmm. Maybe we should call him and invite him to join us tomorrow," Bailey said.

As the girls picked up Mrs. Howell's purse, Alex noticed a "house" phone near the front desk—a phone for guests to use to call the hotel rooms. She punched in the operator's number and asked for Angelo's room.

No one picked up in Angelo's room. She left him a message and told him to meet them at the bus stop if he was interested. Then they headed up to the room.

The girls got back in the elevator talking about their plans for the next day. When they got off the elevator, they could already hear the commotion coming from their room at the end of the hallway. To Alexis's surprise, a hotel manager was standing at their door, knocking. She and Bailey stood slightly behind him to see what was going on as Mrs. Howell opened the door.

"Yes? Can I help you?" she said.

"Yes, ma'am," said the manager. "I wonder if you could have your little ones calm down a bit? It's just that we've had a number of complaints from your floor—"

"Oh, I'm so sorry—"

"And the floor below you—"

"Sir, I promise they won't—"

"*And* the floor above you as well," the man finished.

Alexis's mother looked sorry, but Alexis could tell that underneath she was furious. Not at the manager, but at her twin sons.

"Thank you, sir," she said through clenched teeth. "It won't happen again." The man smiled and walked back toward the elevator. Alexis barely caught the door before it closed, and she and Bailey made it into the room just in time to hear the melee that ensued.

"I told you two to settle down!" Mrs. Howell was yelling. "If I have to tell you again, you're not skiing tomorrow! I'll sign you up for the hotel day care instead, and you can play with the two-year-olds! I'm not kidding!"

Alexis and Bailey sat down with Mr. Howell on the couch. He was watching the Discovery Channel and checking e-mail, completely unaware of the chaos in the bedroom.

"It's hard to believe you two could make it onto real-life TV!" he said to Alexis and Bailey. "How's the filming coming anyway?"

"Really well," said Alexis. She told him all about the baby bats and the sick coyotes. She even told him about the bear cave and the one that woke up, though she failed to mention how close she and Bailey had been when it happened.

Ding!

A small screen popped up on Mr. Howell's laptop.

"Here, Alex. Looks like you've got an e-mail," he said, handing her the computer. From the next room over, they heard a lamp crash to the floor.

"I'd better go help your mother," laughed Mr. Howell, and he left them alone on the couch.

Bailey got so excited that she almost knocked the computer to the floor. "It couldn't be Kate, could it? It's too soon!"

"Let's see," said Alexis, and she opened up the e-mail.

Alex and Bailey,

It's so great to hear from you, and it's SUPER great to know that I can help you! Pulling a pic out of that vid was easy. You'll find the pics attached to this e-mail. I gave you what you asked for—close-ups of the guy on the snowmobile, but I zoomed in a little more for a

*few pics I thought might help you more. You'll see
what I mean. Love you lots! Happy investigating,
and don't hesitate to call if you need me again!*

Kate

Alexis hurried to open the files. There were four
of them. The first was a picture of the whole scene:
a man bundled up from head to toe climbing onto a
snowmobile. They couldn't see his face, but they could
see what he was carrying over his shoulder.

"Is that a gun?" asked Bailey.

"Probably a BB gun," said Alexis. She opened the
next picture.

It was a close-up of the man's face, but it was fully
covered with a ski mask. That didn't help much. The
third picture was just of the snowmobile, and the
fourth was a super close-up of the side of the vehicle.

"Why would she send us that?" asked Bailey. The
computer bounced on Alexis's lap as Mr. Howell sat
back down on the couch.

"Oh!" he said. "A Yamaha Phazer! Those are great
snowmobiles. Super expensive, though. You two
interested in riding?"

"You could say that," said Alexis. She was staring
at the make and model of the snowmobile, trying to

figure out why Kate had zoomed in far enough to see it. All of a sudden, it hit her.

"Bailey, this is huge! We may not have his face, but we know what kind of snowmobile he was driving! Maybe that will lead us to who he is!"

"Maybe," said Bailey. "But it's not like this is *CSI*. We don't have access to all of the registered snowmobile owners in California. And even if we did, how would we know which one was this guy?"

"You're right, Bailey. This isn't *CSI*, but we can still use the info. Didn't you hear Dad? These things are expensive. I bet whoever was riding it rented it. Tomorrow we can call around to the rental places in town and see if anyone took out a Yamaha Phazer today. That's a start anyway. Then we'll go investigate the area near the cave again. Maybe this guy left something behind."

When the girls climbed into bed, Alexis couldn't fall asleep. Bailey's light snoring wasn't keeping her up. Her mind was. It seemed to be going about a million miles per hour. She hoped this snowmobile would lead them to whoever was sabotaging the reserve. She knew it could be a dead end, but she refused to think about that right now.

Please, God, she prayed. *Help us tomorrow. We need a break. The reserve needs You. We need You. This is where the real investigating begins.*

Starstruck

The next morning, the girls awoke to a wall of white. Snowflakes as big as silver dollars drifted toward the ground—so many that they melded together to form a frozen fog. There had always been snow on the ground since they arrived, but at least four more feet had fallen while they slept.

Alexis looked out the window and felt like she had landed on another planet.

"I hope we're not stuck in the hotel today!" squealed Bailey from behind her.

"Me, too," said Alexis.

"One thing's for sure," she continued, layering on her thick socks and snow boots. "Even if we can get to the reserve, there's no way we'll be able to examine the site near the bear cave. Any evidence will be covered up."

Alexis and Bailey weren't too hopeful as they rode the elevator down to the lobby. They were surprised to see that it was business as usual outside. Cars and buses chugged by the hotel. Bundled-up tourists trudged into the corner coffee shop. The only things out of place were the huge piles of snow on the sides of the street. Every few minutes a huge snowplow roared its way through. It pushed the newly fallen snow out of the street, adding to the piles.

As the girls waited to see if the bus would come, they didn't see any sign of Angelo. The bus picked them up as usual, though now there were metal chains clacking on all of its four wheels. Lisa picked them up in the jeep. A small plow was sticking out of its front bumper. It took much longer than usual to traverse the road to the reserve office. Every once in a while, Lisa had to let the plow down to push through the snowdrifts.

"You're really good at that," said Bailey from the backseat.

"Thanks," said Lisa. "Thankfully this only happens a few times a year. I don't know what we'd do if we had to deal with it all the time!"

"I even saw a school bus on our way here," said Alexis. "My cousin in Tennessee gets out of school if they *think* it's going to snow! Wait until I tell her that kids in Tahoe go in a blizzard!"

"Yeah," laughed Lisa. "It takes a lot to get a snow day here."

By the time they were inside the office, warming themselves by the fire, Jake and Karen were already doing their rounds with the animals.

"Hey, Lisa?" Alexis said. "We have a lot of video of the animals. Do you think we could interview you about the reserve and your parents?"

"Sure!" said Lisa. "I finished a lot of my work early this morning. Besides, if you two win, I'll be on TV! And I'm *sure* you'll win. You just have to! People will love this."

Alexis spent the next hour behind the camera filming as Bailey asked Lisa question after question. They learned everything they could about the reserve. Lisa's grandparents had started it with their life savings, and the Ingles had worked continually to expand it since then. It was the only reserve of its kind in California or Nevada—the only option for the animals that animal control and the humane society couldn't deal with.

The Ingleses felt their setup was still too small. Just last month they had had to turn away a wolf that someone had tried to keep as a pet. They just didn't have the space. The wolf had gone to a sanctuary near Olympia in Washington State, but he had been lucky—most animals Karen and Jake couldn't keep had nowhere else to go. If a zoo couldn't take them, they had to be released or put to sleep.

After the interview, Lisa had to leave. The local high school was having a college fair, and she was going to help answer questions about her university. Before she left, Alexis caught her at the door.

"Lisa?" she called into the snow. "Do you think we could use the phone for a bunch of local calls? We were going to follow up on a lead."

"Sure! Mom and Dad will be busy until lunch anyway."

Alexis got out her pink notebook and placed it next to the phone while Bailey scrounged around the office looking for the phone book. There was a whole page full of numbers for snowmobile rentals, so the girls decided to go in alphabetical order.

By the time Alexis had called half the rental places, she still hadn't written anything down. Bailey was getting bored. She started making origami out of a pile of yellow sticky notes lying on the desk.

Finally, on about the twentieth call, they got a break. Alexis learned that the snowmobile they were looking for was rare because it was expensive. Only two places in South Tahoe even rented them—and one of those places was only minutes away from the reserve! It was called Rainbow Rentals.

"This makes sense, Bailey!" said Alexis. "If the person we're looking for rented the snowmobile just down the road, they wouldn't have had to transport it at all. They could have just taken off up the mountain and circled around onto the reserve's property! Bailey! Are you even listening?"

Bailey's head had drooped onto the desk. She was sleeping comfortably and drooling on a half-made paper bird. Alexis shook her.

"Bailey!"

"Huh? What?" Bailey said. She sat up and Alexis laughed. One of Bailey's sticky-note creations had stuck to her cheek.

"I might have found the right place," said Alexis. "I just need to make one more call to check."

Alexis made the call and scribbled furiously on her notebook the whole time. It turned out that someone *had* rented a Yamaha Phazer the day before. It was a girl who rented the machine all the time. Her name was Chloe. She had long, red hair and was a bit of a snob according to the guy on the phone. Alexis thanked him for the information and hung up.

"So, do you think this Chloe girl is the one who is doing all of this damage?" asked Bailey.

"If she rented the snowmobile, then she might be

the one waking the bears," said Alexis. "But we still have to figure out who she is and tie her to the crimes if we're going to get her to stop. That's what has to happen before the reserve will be safe."

Bailey opened her mouth to say something else, but nothing came out. She was staring over Alexis's shoulder at the front door to the office. Her mouth was hanging open, and when Alexis asked her what was wrong, she just pointed toward the door. Alexis turned around, and it was all she could do to keep her mouth from dropping open as well.

Standing in the doorway was none other than Misty Marks, one of Hollywood's most popular actresses. Miss Marks shrugged off her coat and hung it on the rack, just as if she were at home. Then she turned to the girls.

"Hello!" she said, crossing the room. "I don't believe I've met you two. I'm Misty, Karen's sister."

Alexis shook Misty's hand.

"Oh, hello," she said. "I'm Alexis and this is Bailey."

Alexis elbowed her friend, and Bailey finally closed her mouth.

"You still have a bird stuck to your face!" Alexis whispered. Bailey swiped at her cheek and sent the paper pigeon flying across the room. It landed near

Bubbles, startling him awake. Misty Marks looked like she was trying not to laugh.

"Are you two new here at the reserve?" she asked.

"Oh no," said Alexis. "I mean, yes! Well, we don't work here or anything. We're shooting a documentary for a contest."

"That's right! My sister told me about that! Is she around?"

Just then, Karen burst through the back door.

"Misty! I thought I heard your car!" The two women hugged, and then they both began talking at the same time. Bailey leaned toward Alexis.

"Karen's sister is *Misty Marks*?" she said. Alexis just nodded. How exciting! Alexis *loved* movies, and here she was meeting one of the hottest stars in Hollywood. It was obvious that Bailey was even more excited. She simply couldn't sit still.

"So, Misty, have you met our detectives?" asked Karen.

"Detectives? I thought they were filming a documentary."

"Yes, they are, but Alexis and Bailey have offered to help us figure out what is behind all of the strange happenings here," said Karen.

"Well, not really what," said Bailey. "It's actually a *who*."

"Really?" said Misty. "How interesting! Any leads?"

The actress leaned down toward the desk to get closer. Alexis was surprised. She had always thought that movie stars would all be rude in real life. Apparently Misty Marks was really interested in their mystery.

"Well, we did figure out who rented the snowmobile we saw yesterday. We think this girl could be the one who woke up the bear," said Alexis.

"*And* the one who shot Alexis with a BB gun!" said Bailey.

"What?" said Karen. "Someone *shot* you?"

"Well, we didn't know it at the time, but my dad said my bruise was caused by a BB. See?" Alexis pointed at the blotchy bruise on her right cheek.

"And we think that's how the person woke up the bear. She was shooting BBs into the cave."

"This is a lot more serious than you made it sound, Karen," said Misty. "I thought you all had just forgotten to lock the cages a couple of times."

"That's what we thought, too," said Jake. He was at the back door stomping snow from his boots and shaking it out of his hair. "Hi, Misty. Good to see you."

"You, too, Jake," said Misty. "So what's really going on?"

"Well, we thought everything was falling apart and that it was all our fault," said Karen. "But then these girls showed up, and we realized that someone is sabotaging us. We found chocolate wrappers near the coyote cages the day they got sick, so we think someone fed them chocolate to purposely make them sick. And we think someone has been sneaking our keys and letting out animals. And just yesterday someone woke up a brown bear out of hibernation."

"How is the bear?" asked Alexis. "Did you find him?"

"Oh yeah," said Jake. "We tranquilized him and took him back to the cave. Hopefully when he wakes up, he'll realize he's comfortable and go back to sleep."

"Speaking of getting comfortable, let's go sit down and talk about this for a few minutes," Karen said. She led the group to the couches, and everyone sat around the fire.

"Alexis," Karen said. "I'm worried. You could have really gotten hurt. What if that BB had hit you in the eye?"

"She got hit by a BB?" asked Jake, and Alexis told her story all over again. She could see Jake was getting angry, so before he could suggest that she and Bailey stop investigating, she told him about the snowmobile and the "Chloe" girl they thought was responsible.

"We're getting close to figuring this out, Jake," said Bailey. "It won't take too long now."

"Okay," said Jake. "So you know that a girl named

Chloe rented the snowmobile. How are you going to find her? Do you even know where to start looking?"

Alexis hadn't thought that far ahead yet. Tahoe was a big place, and her dad wasn't just going to let her and Bailey wander around it looking for some girl with red hair.

"We'll just have to pray for another clue that leads us in the right direction," said Alexis. She smiled her most confident smile.

"Well, I guess we already know it's not a tourist or any of our environmentalist groups," said Jake.

"Really?" said Bailey. "How do we know that?"

"Well, the environmentalists usually ride around town on bicycles. They're not really the type to rent a top-of-the-line snowmobile. And a tourist wouldn't have known where to find the bear caves."

Jake was right. Alexis's head was spinning. What did this mean? Whoever was doing this was probably a resident—someone who lived in the Tahoe area. Either that, or they were very familiar with it. What she and Bailey really needed was another clue. A *real* one that would point them in the right direction.

Laughter interrupted Alexis's thoughts. The group's conversation had shifted. Now they were talking about Bruce Benton, the rich guy from the resort.

"Yeah," Misty was saying, "I ran into him at breakfast, and he wanted me to remind you how far all that money could go. He really thinks this mountain would be the perfect place for an upscale resort. It's on the quiet side of town, away from all of the noise and gambling over in Stateline. He's right, you know—"

"*What?*" said Jake. "You really think I should sell my family's heritage to that no-good, slimy—"

"No, no! Jake, let me finish," said Misty. Alexis was amazed. Jake had all but yelled at the actress, and Misty Marks was still smiling her Oscar-winning smile. It was like there was a joke that no one knew about but her.

"What I was *going* to say, Jake, is that he's right about the location. It would make a great resort, but there are plenty of resorts around this lake. I reminded him that this was the only reserve of its kind in the area. And it's in a great central location to serve both California *and* Nevada. Even if you did want to sell, it would be almost impossible to find another tract of land this perfectly suited to what you do."

"Oh. Well, thank you, Misty," said Jake. "Sorry about before. I've been a little on edge lately."

Alexis was lost in thought again. So Bruce Benton wanted the reserve, huh? Hadn't she and Bailey heard him discussing his new resort the other day? He had said there were some complications. . .but he had also said that they wouldn't last long.

Was it possible? Could this Bruce guy be involved in sabotaging the reserve just so he could have the land? It *was* a very "Cruella" thing to do. Alexis scribbled a reminder in her notebook. She would talk to Bailey about her idea as soon as they were alone again.

"Well," said Misty, bringing Alexis back to the conversation again. "It looks like everyone needs to get back to work. How would you girls like to hear *my* take on all of this?"

"You mean like an interview?" asked Alexis.

"Sure! If you need it, that is. I don't have a lot of time, but I'm willing."

"It would be great to have an outside perspective on the hard work Karen and Jake have put into the reserve. Bailey? Would you like to take the camera and interview Miss Marks?"

Bailey was speechless again, but a huge smile broke her face almost in two.

CHAPTER 8

Out Cold

Bailey chattered away as she dug the tripod out of Alexis's camera bag. The thought of interviewing one of her favorite actresses had finally loosened her tongue, and now she was asking Misty Marks about a million questions a minute. Misty just laughed as she followed Bailey into the back office. It would give them a quiet place to conduct most of the interview.

Alexis decided it would also be a good idea to get scenes of Bailey and Misty walking around the reserve. "I'll set up the camera and let you two get started with the interview. Since Misty's time is limited, while you're doing the interview, I'm going to find some areas where we can have good shots of you two to show. Then we'll edit it all together later."

"Sounds great to me," Misty said, flashing another of her famous smiles.

Before Alexis shut the door, Bailey looked back and waved at her.

"Thank you!" she mouthed. Alexis gave her two thumbs-up and smiled. She wondered if the actress would get a word in.

Alexis sat back on the couch and got out her notebook. As she looked over her notes about the mysterious "Chloe," Bubbles jumped up onto the cushion next to her and put his head in her lap. His misty eyes looked up into hers like he was asking her for something. Alexis looked at Karen nervously.

"He may be three times bigger, Alexis, but sometimes Bubbles thinks he's just a plain ol' house cat. I think he wants you to pet him."

Alexis rubbed Bubbles's head. The little tufts of hair sticking out from the tips of his ears were extremely soft. She realized that long tufts stuck out from between each of his toes as well. Alexis could see how people might think a bobcat would make an awesome pet. It was like holding a giant kitten. . .until Bubbles yawned and reminded her that his teeth were much bigger.

Jake was walking back toward the couch with two steaming mugs of coffee when they heard it—a muffled cough from somewhere outside and a faint rattle.

"Is someone outside?" asked Karen. "I thought I heard a cough."

"Shh!" said Jake. He was frozen in the middle of the room, his head bent toward the sound. "It's not the cough I'm worried about. It's the can of spray paint!"

He dropped both cups of coffee and bolted out the back door. Karen and Alexis stared at each other for a minute before following. They ran to the back steps just in time to see Jake disappear around the corner of the building.

"Be careful, Jake!" Karen called. There wasn't a path through the snow here, so Alexis and Karen waited under the eave.

"He won't catch them," said Karen. "He never does."

They stood in silence for a minute. Then for two. Then almost five had gone by, and they hadn't heard anything. Karen took off through the snow calling after Jake. Alexis followed again, tripping through the feet of loose powder. They rounded the corner, and Alexis saw the paint. The messy, red letters stood out against the snow like spaghetti sauce spilled on a new, white shirt.

Get Out While You Can.

The last letter trailed off at the end, as if the painter had been caught before finishing.

"Jake?" Karen called again. Still there was no answer. The women left the first barn and circled around so they were near the outside edge of the parking lot. As they rounded another corner, Karen stopped so suddenly that Alexis ran into her.

"Jake! Oh no!"

Karen stumbled through the snow and knelt on the ground. Alexis came up behind Karen and gasped. Jake was lying in the snow, unconscious. At first Alexis thought the dark red all over his face was paint. Had the mysterious painter sprayed Jake in the face so he could get away? Then it hit her.

It wasn't paint. It was blood.

"Jake! Jake!" Karen said. She was wiping blood away from his mouth and nose. Jake opened his eyes. He sat up and looked frantically around.

"Did you see him? Did you see the car?"

"What? No," said Karen. "You were alone when we got here. Out cold. What happened?"

"I saw the guy painting the barn and tried to catch him. He must have waited for me around this corner, because when I rounded it, his fist was there waiting. I never saw a thing—just his black coat."

Alexis left Karen's side and walked toward the parking lot. A series of footprints led her through the parking lot to the other side where tire tracks showed where the person's car must have been parked. Near the parking spot, two things caught her eye—the can of spray paint was on the ground, and something red glinted on the bark of a nearby tree. Alexis took a step closer and saw a large handprint in red paint.

It was too big to be a woman's hand. And a woman had probably not hit Jake hard enough to knock him out and mess up his face like that. So if "Chloe" didn't paint the barn, who did? Were the two connected? Or were there many different people out to mess with Karen and Jake and ruin their reserve?

Alexis made her way back to Karen, who was helping Jake up the front steps and into the office. Inside, Bailey was helping Misty Marks clean up the broken coffee mugs. Alexis noticed that the puddle of liquid was no longer steaming.

"What happened, Karen?" asked Misty. "We heard you yell. Oh Jake! What happened to your face?"

As Karen told her sister the story, Alexis went to the small kitchen and filled a bag with ice from the freezer. When she got back to the couch, she handed it to Jake, who had just hung up the phone.

"Thanks, kid," he said. Jake laid his head on the back of the couch and balanced the bag of ice on his throbbing nose and cheek. "The police said it will take them quite awhile to get here—with the weather, they have a lot of accidents they have to get to first."

"Oh no, Jake! What about the benefit? You can't get on stage with your face looking like that!" Misty exclaimed.

"Misty," Jake laughed, "I think a flashy party is the least of our worries right now, don't you? Maybe we should think about canceling it anyway. What if word gets out that we're having these problems?"

"Jake, we can't afford to cancel the benefit," said Karen. "It's our number-one source for donations all year!"

"What benefit?" asked Alexis.

"Did you say a flashy party?" asked Bailey. Her eyes lit up, and she scooted to the edge of the couch.

"Well, yes," said Karen. "Every year we have a benefit party at one of the resorts. This year it's at the one you're staying in. People come from all over the country to hear what we've been doing and what we plan to do in the next year. Then they donate the money that helps us run this place. We were hoping that this year we would get enough to expand—maybe even enough to build our own animal hospital and to hire a vet."

"Yes, it's a tradition!" chimed Misty. "And Karen's right, Jake. You can't afford to cancel the benefit. It's tomorrow night! People are already in town just for you!"

Alexis saw the light in Misty's eyes and figured she was the reason for most of the donations made to the reserve. If Alexis was right, there would be more than one movie star at that party. By the look of awe on Bailey's face, she had the same idea. Misty noticed, too.

"I have an idea!" she said. "How about if we invite our movie makers to the party! They can film some of it for their documentary. . . *and* get to meet some really cool people!"

"That's a great idea!" said Karen.

"I don't know," said Jake. "Haven't we gotten them in enough trouble?"

"It won't be an issue, Jake," said Misty. "The party's at their hotel this year! They won't even have to go anywhere."

The girls sat on the edge of the couch, leaning toward Jake. Alexis tried not to look too excited, but the idea of being in a room full of stars had her head spinning.

"All right," said Jake with a smile. Bailey and Misty squealed together and then immediately began talking of dresses and high heels. Alexis was excited, but her mind went in another direction. She was thinking about the spray paint and the red handprint again. She and Bailey *had* to solve this case, because it wouldn't matter how much money was donated to the reserve if the government shut it down.

Alexis went over all of the clues in her mind. There had to be something she was missing—somewhere they hadn't looked. And then it hit her.

"The letters!" she said, startling everyone in the room.

"What d'you mean, Lexi?" asked Bailey. "What letters?"

"The threatening letters Karen and Jake have been getting—we haven't looked at them yet. Jake, do you think we could browse through them?"

"Sure, Alexis. They're in the top drawer of the desk."

Alexis and Bailey sat behind the desk again like they had that morning making phone calls. Alexis spread about twelve letters out in front of them. A few were old and wrinkled and looked as though they had been made out of old newspapers. The newest ones, however, were very different. Their words weren't cut from dull gray newspaper. Instead, they were shiny or glossy, like a magazine.

Alexis prodded the edge of one of the glued words and realized that, unlike a magazine, the paper was thick—almost like cardstock, the heavy paper used for index cards, menus, and other things that need heavier paper.

"Look, there's a picture on the other side of that word! That's a picture of our hotel!" shouted Bailey. Sure enough, as Alex pulled the word up, the back side of it showed the stone tower and part of the hotel's title in lights. Bailey was right!

"Bailey," said Alexis, "I think these letters are made out of brochures! Pamphlets advertising hotels around Tahoe!"

By this time, the others had gathered around the desk to look over the girls' shoulders.

"I think you're right," said Karen. "Look—this is Harrah's!"

"And this one's from Caesar's," said Jake. "These are the most recent letters we've gotten. What could this mean?"

"I'm not sure," said Alexis. "But it narrows things down. Whoever is bothering you guys must hang around the resorts, where it's obviously easy for them to get their hands on these brochures."

Alexis pulled out her camera and started taking pictures of the brochures.

A horn honked from outside.

"That's Lisa," said Jake. "Time for you all to get back to the hotel. We'll be in touch about the party."

The girls smiled and said their good-byes. The

bus ride back was quiet. Both Bailey and Alexis were thinking about the new clues they had. What did "Chloe" and the snowmobile have to do with the brochures and the man with the red spray paint? Were they connected? Alexis looked out the window into the wall of white and pleaded with the One she knew could help them piece together the puzzle.

Please, God! We need a break. We have all of these clues but no way to connect them.

When the girls got back to the hotel, they zoomed straight to Mrs. Howell's laptop. Alexis uploaded the photos of the letters and posted them on the CCG website. Then she started writing in the CCG chat wall. She told the girls about the threatening letters and about the message in the red spray paint, as well as the handprint.

Soon the girls were responding to her words.

> Sydney: *Did you find anything out about who was renting the snowmobile?*
> Alexis: *Sounds like some woman named Chloe.*
> McKenzie: *Do you think she's the one who left the message in the snow and knocked out Jake?*
> Alexis: *No, Bailey pointed out that the*

101

*handprint is too big for most women—
unless she's a real amazon. And it would take
quite a punch to knock out Jake. Karen
thinks from the way the injury looks that
the person did it with his knuckles, not with
any weapon.*

Kate: *Unless she's an amazon and a wrestler
or something, too! Or a policewoman! They
learn how to pack punches.*

Sydney: *Well, if the words on the letters look
like they're all on Lake Tahoe brochures,
you're probably right about it being someone who's hanging around the resort area.*

Kate: *Although any public place sixty miles
around Lake Tahoe probably has racks of
brochures promoting their attractions.*

Alexis: *Yeah, they do, but I just have a feeling
it's someone who hangs around the resorts.
It's definitely someone who's familiar with
the reserve—enough to even know where the
bears sleep.*

Elizabeth: *I think you should go with that gut
feeling. I think it's God directing you.*

Alexis: *Well, He'd better direct fast. Bailey
and I feel like we've hit a dead end, and we*

only have a couple of days left here.

McKenzie: *Don't be discouraged. I think you're way closer to solving this than you were twenty-four hours ago.*

Elizabeth: *Yes, you've learned that the person sending them hangs out around the resorts, probably.*

Sydney: *And the spray painter made a big mistake by leaving a handprint. And since most spray paint is permanent, it will probably be a few days before he—assuming it's a he—can get the paint off his hand.*

Alexis: *So all we have to do is go around asking if we can see every man's hand?*

McKenzie: *Well, let's hope it doesn't come to that. . . .*

Elizabeth: *But whatever it takes! LOL!*

Sydney: *Yeah! If you keep your eyes open, you'll catch him.*

Alexis: *You're right. We'll even catch the criminal red-handed! Literally! ROTFL.*

A Redhead Red-Handed?

Before dinnertime Alexis and Bailey took to the streets. Their goal was to watch people, and they were looking for something very specific. Jake had mentioned that the painter had been wearing a black coat. They were looking for someone who looked like he had money—since he hung around at the resorts all day, and they weren't cheap—and who had an obvious red stain on his hand.

Soon, however, they hit a roadblock. They found that, on the Nevada side of the state line, they couldn't go *inside* any of the hotels. All of them had casinos on the ground floors, and Alexis and Bailey were obviously not old enough to walk around those without parents.

"That's all right," said Bailey after they had been shown politely out of their third casino. "It's nasty in there anyway. . .all smoky, and it's hard to hear myself think over the blinging noises of all those crazy machines!"

Bailey was right. Alexis hadn't enjoyed being inside the casinos, but she also knew that they didn't have much of a chance of finding who they were looking for if they were limited to walking the sidewalks.

The snow started picking up, swirling thick around their heads. Bailey spoke up again.

"What if he's wearing gloves, Lexi? We won't be able to see his hands if he's wearing gloves."

Alexis hated to admit it, but Bailey was right. After more than an hour, Alexis led Bailey back to their hotel. They sat down in the lobby in front of the big fire to thaw out a little and talk about what to do next. The only other person nearby was a young woman using a laptop computer. She was wearing a scarf over her head, so Alexis guessed she had just come in from outside, too.

The girls chatted, until the woman's phone rang. She picked it up with a huff and answered it stiffly.

"Chloe Stevens, how may I help you?"

Alexis and Bailey froze when they heard the name. They sat very still and eavesdropped, pretending to watch the fire dance in the hearth.

"No, he is unavailable tomorrow night," snapped the woman named Chloe. "In fact, he won't be in the office until next week. Yes. Thank you."

She hung up the phone and went back to her computer. After less than a minute, her phone rang again. The woman tore the scarf off her head in frustration, and Alexis gasped.

The woman's hair was bright red.

Alexis looked at Bailey, and it was obvious that Bailey was thinking the same thing. They had found "Chloe," and they hadn't even been looking for her! Alexis waited patiently for Chloe to finish her phone call, and then she began a conversation.

"So, are you enjoying your stay in Tahoe?" asked Alexis. "Are you on vacation?"

Chloe looked up from her computer, surprised to be addressed by two young strangers.

"No, and no," she said. Then she lowered her head to the computer screen again. Alexis wasn't turned off by Chloe's obvious attempt to ignore her. She pressed on.

"Done anything fun, though? Skiing? Snowmobiling?"

Chloe made a disgusted sound.

"Ugh, no! I hate the snow. I can't wait to get out of this place and get back to the Valley." The phone rang again. Chloe snapped her laptop closed and stood up quickly.

"Thanks for the conversation," she said rudely, "but

I'm going to bed. It's the only way to get away from the boss who never stops calling."

With that, she stormed off toward the elevators and was gone.

"I guess that wasn't her," said Bailey. "You heard her. She hates the snow. Some other red-haired Chloe must have rented the snowmobile."

"Hmm, maybe," said Alexis. She wasn't convinced. She didn't believe in coincidences, and it would be a huge one if there were two young redheaded "Chloes" walking around the small town of South Lake Tahoe. The good thing was that it seemed like Chloe must be staying at their hotel. If she were somehow connected to the painter, they would probably find him here as well.

She couldn't help but feel that God had answered her prayer on the bus. He was leading them closer to the answer, she just *knew* it. Before she could say what she was thinking, Bailey nudged her arm.

"Look, Lexi. Several computers are empty. Let's go see if the Camp Club Girls have found out anything."

The girls walked to a huge column that was surrounded by computers and chairs. FOR PATRONS' CONVENIENCE, the sign above each computer read. Alexis knew that this was a hotel where a lot of companies and organizations held conventions, like her dad's company. She'd seen people dash out between meetings to check their messages. She knew from being around her mom and dad that they were making sure nothing important had popped up at work while they were in the meetings.

So Alexis felt rather important sitting down and logging in to the Camp Club Girls' website. She felt almost like an adult dashing to get the latest news from her coworkers in solving mysteries and mayhem.

She and Bailey started to read the messages on the chat wall together.

> Sydney: *You know, girls, I've been thinking about the woman named Chloe who rented the snowmobile. Even if she didn't KO Jake, I have a feeling she might be involved in this.*
> Alexis: *That's amazing. Just wait until you hear WHOM we just sat next to in the hotel lobby.*

Alex took a few minutes to explain what they'd seen and heard from the woman next to them.

> Sydney: *Well even if she doesn't like snow, she still could have rented the snowmobile for*

her boss. Assistants do that kind of thing, you know.

McKenzie: *If I were you, I'd try to follow her until you know for sure that it's not the Chloe you're looking for. I think Sydney's right. I have a feeling about her, too.*

Elizabeth: *She sounds like she might lead you to bigger fish, as we say here in Texas.*

Alexis: *Bigger fish?*

Elizabeth: *Yes. The person who's really at the helm of the dastardly deeds.*

Sydney: *If she is the right Chloe, she might lead you to the person who's really responsible for sabotaging the reserve.*

McKenzie: *I've also been thinking about your new friend, Angelo.*

Alexis: *You think he did this stuff? But he's blind, Kenz. I don't think he could have ridden a snowmobile. I guess he could have written with paint in the snow, but I don't think it would be as legible. . . .*

McKenzie: *No, silly. Bailey's been up here in Montana, so she can tell you how many mountains we have in parts of our state. Some people from my church have a ministry helping people with disabilities do sports things, like participating in rodeos and even skiing.*

Elizabeth: *How do they do that?*

McKenzie: *People who can see and help skiers get around are called guides. They ski the trail with the blind person and help him or her avoid obstacles and learn the course.*

Elizabeth: *That must be a really hard thing to do.*

McKenzie: *They say it's not as hard as people think. Although blind people don't have their sight and can't follow a guide with their eyes, they can follow the guide with their ears and other senses. And they tend to have good instincts that help them find their way around.*

Alexis: *Really? Do they have friends who help people around here?*

McKenzie: *Well, no, I don't think so. But I went online and looked up the resort where you're staying. They're having a ski meet in a couple of days. I e-mailed them to see if people with disabilities can compete, and they told me yes. I told them about your friend, Angelo, and they said they had guides available to help at the meet. The guides give the people with disabilities a little bit of help so they can compete. All Angelo has to do is register for the meet and request one ahead of time. He just needs to talk to Mark at extension 378 in the resort.*

Alexis: *Terrific! I'll make sure he knows that!*

McKenzie: *The guy named Mark was really nice. He said if you guys had any questions to just ask him.*

Bailey nudged Alexis's shoulder. "Look, Angelo just walked by. He's sitting over there. Maybe we should go talk to him about it."

"Good idea," Alexis said as she typed their good-byes to their online friends and logged out of the public computer.

As the girls approached Angelo, they saw that his eyebrows were crumpled into a scowl.

Bailey said. "Hey, Angelo! Over here!"

The boy's face lit up as he turned toward the girls.

"What's up, Angelo? You look bummed," said Alexis.

"Well, it's not a big deal," said Angelo. "I found out about a ski race the resort's sponsoring later this week.

I just wish I could be part of it."

"But you can!" Bailey exclaimed.

"We told one of our friends about meeting you the other day and how you wished you could ski," Alexis explained.

Bailey picked up the story. "She contacted the hotel and talked to a guy named Mark at extension 378."

"He said they have guides for skiers who need help!" Alexis said. "All you have to do is call him to register and to request a guide."

"That's awesome, Angelo! You should totally enter!" cried Bailey.

"Hey, you can do it right now!" Alexis exclaimed, noticing the house phone nearby.

"Well, I guess I could," Angelo said hesitantly.

"Here, we'll help!" The girls led Angelo to a bench by the phone. They sat beside him as he punched in the extension number 378.

The girls listened to Angelo sign up.

"Okay," he said. "Do you have anyone who can help me practice? . . . Oh, I see. . . . Well, yes, let's go ahead and leave me signed up for the event. Maybe I can figure something out."

Angelo sighed heavily as he hung up the receiver and leaned back in his chair.

"Is there a problem?" Alexis asked.

"Well, a bit of a challenge." Angelo smiled weakly. "They have guides to help at the race, and I'm signed up for one. But they don't have any practice guides available. I need to practice if I'm going to compete. Oh well."

Alexis could tell he was trying not to kill the mood and depress everyone else. She thought hard for a minute, and then her eyes lit up.

"Angelo! I've got an idea!" she said. "Meet us tomorrow morning at the ski lodge—as soon as the lifts open!"

"But, Alexis—"

"No buts! Just do it! And be ready to practice!" Alexis jumped off the couch and grabbed Bailey by the arm.

"Come on, Bailey! We have a lot to do before tomorrow!" The girls took off toward the elevators, leaving Angelo baffled but smiling in the lobby.

•—•—•

The next morning, Alexis and Bailey waited impatiently for Angelo to show up. They still had half an hour before the slopes opened, but Alexis was excited. She wanted to get started right away. She had spent most of the last evening getting what she needed from the rental shop. Then she had called Mark at extension 378 and talked to him. He had explained what to do and had told her that all she needed besides skis and poles were two vests.

One was for Angelo. It was orange, and it said BLIND SKIER in black. Alexis's vest was orange as well. It said GUIDE. Alexis was already in her vest when Angelo came around the corner with his skis.

"Good morning, ladies!" he chimed. "So what's the plan?"

"First, you have to put this on," said Bailey. She tossed the vest into Angelo's chest, and he caught it easily.

"Sweet!" said Angelo. "If you're giving me a vest for practicing, you must have found me a practice guide? Who is it? I thought they were all busy."

"They are all busy," said Alexis. "I'm the one who's going to lead you through the course. Mark at extension 378 and the guy in the ski shop walked me through what to do and gave me the vests. He said he remembered you from when you were here skiing with your dad before. He said you probably wouldn't need a guide for long, anyway, because you're so good."

Angelo looked more than a little nervous.

"Have you ever done this before, Alexis?" he asked.

"No. But I'm sure we'll do great! Come on!"

Alexis led Bailey and Angelo to the ski lift that took them to the top of the race course. More than once, she tried to help Angelo when he didn't really need it.

"The chair's almost here. Get ready to sit."

"I know, Alexis. I can hear it," Angelo teased. Alexis had to remind herself that Angelo had skied much more than she had. If he'd known the race course already, he wouldn't even have needed her.

Their first time down the course, Alexis realized just how good Angelo was. She weaved slowly in and out of the blue flags that made up the course, calling back to him only to say "left" or "right." After three times through, Angelo was simply following the sound of Alexis skiing ahead of him. Bailey stayed behind them, taking her time.

"Okay, Alexis!" Angelo called. "You can speed up now! I should practice going fast."

"I'm going almost as fast as I can!" Alexis called back. "I've never done a race course before today, and I'm not a good skier to begin with!" As if to demonstrate her last claim, Alexis took the final turn on the race course, and her skies got tangled. She did a rolling dive down the rest of the hill and came to a stop near the end of the lift lines. Bailey and Angelo caught up, barely holding in their laughter.

"Are you okay, Lexi?" asked Bailey.

"Yeah, I'm fine. I'll be a little sore, but nothing too bad."

"Thanks a lot for your help, Alexis," said Angelo.

"I'll be fine tomorrow. My race guide will take me through a couple practice runs in the morning. I know the turns by heart, and that's the main thing."

"Are you sure, Angelo?" asked Alexis. "I don't feel like we did much."

"It was perfect," said Angelo. He kicked off his skis and held out a hand to help Alexis up. "If it weren't for you, I wouldn't be able to enter the race at all. You two will come watch tomorrow, right?"

"We wouldn't miss it for the world!" said Bailey.

"Good. I'll see you both in the morning! Have fun at your fancy party!" Angelo picked up his skis and made his way back up to the lodge.

Bailey was smiling ear to ear, but when she looked at Alexis, she scowled.

"What's wrong, Lexi?"

Alexis looked as if the bogeyman had just jumped out at her from under the bed. Her eyes were wide with fear.

"Lexi, what is it?"

"The party!" said Alexis. Her voice came out in a hoarse whisper. "It's tonight!"

"Yeah, it is," said Bailey. "What's the big deal?"

"We don't have anything to wear!"

Within thirty minutes the girls had changed out

of their ski clothes and stuffed down a couple of sandwiches. They left the hotel and walked a couple of blocks away from the state line, passing all kinds of tourist shops.

"The lady at the front desk said there was a great thrift store down here," said Bailey. "It's secondhand, but apparently everything's really nice."

"Good," said Alexis. "I have about thirty dollars for my entire party outfit!"

The thrift store was a gold mine, as far as the girls were concerned. The woman at the register led them to a rack packed full of evening gowns and party dresses.

"Girls don't usually come looking for these until prom," she said to Alexis and Bailey. "That's still a couple months away, so you two have tons to choose from! After you find a dress, the purses and shoes are near the register. Fitting rooms are just through those curtains."

"Thanks," said Alexis. She and Bailey had a blast moving through the racks. There were dresses with feathers and sequins in bright colors, as well as simple black gowns. They all looked as if they could have been worn on the red carpet. Alexis and Bailey each took a small pile into the closest dressing rooms and took turns modeling their choices.

Alexis was trying on a long peach-colored dress when Bailey jumped through the curtain into her dressing room.

"Oh, good," said Alexis. "I need help zipping this up."

"Forget the zipper!" said Bailey. "Look who just walked into the store!"

Alexis poked her head through the curtain and stared. Chloe, the redhead from the hotel, was laughing with the cashier. The woman pointed toward the back of the store, and Alexis dove back into the dressing room as Chloe headed for the dress rack.

"I guess she needs a dress, too," whispered Alexis. "Let's pick our stuff quickly so we can follow her when she leaves!"

Bailey and Alexis tried on the rest of their dresses in a hurry and made their choices on the dresses they liked best. Then they moved to the front of the store to find shoes and accessories. As soon as they had finished, they paid. Then they lingered, pretending to look at jewelry. Alexis kept an eye on Chloe the whole time.

Chloe seemed to be annoyed again. Her phone kept ringing, but she was ignoring it.

"I'm on my lunch break!" she yelled at it when it rang for the seventh time. "Leave me alone!"

"Boss working you too hard, sweetie?" asked the shop owner.

"Not really," answered Chloe as she hung a teal dress back on the rack. "I think he just has something against free time. That's him again, making sure I'm going to be on time for our meeting in twenty minutes."

Soon Chloe checked out at the register. Alexis and Bailey walked outside to wait for her to come out.

"She's going to meet her boss," said Alexis. "This is our chance to see who he is!"

"He could be our guy with the red hand and black coat!" said Bailey. Alexis had a feeling Bailey was right, but she didn't want to get too excited.

At that moment, Chloe came out of the shop and buzzed past them heading back toward the hotels. She was on the phone.

"Yes, sir," she said. "I'm on my way. . . . Yes, your tux-edo for the benefit should be in your room. . . . Yes. . . . Yes, I have my dress. Yes, I'll see you in a few minutes."

She started to put away her phone when the girls heard it sound again. She flipped it open. "Hello? . . . Well, I'm sorry! I told you the paint was permanent. Did you try lemon juice and sugar, like I told you to? . . . Okay then. I don't know if you'll be able to get it off for the event tonight or not. . . . No, you'd look silly in gloves. Try the stuff again, and if it doesn't work, keep your hands in your pockets as much as you can."

She hung up again, and the girls followed at a bit of a distance. They wanted to get a glimpse of Chloe's boss without letting her know she was being followed.

"Oh no!" Alexis said. She grabbed Bailey's arm and pulled her along faster. Chloe was losing them. She had passed the hotel and was headed for a restaurant in one of the casinos.

"No!" cried Bailey. "We can't go in there!"

The girls sped up, hoping they could get a glimpse of the man Chloe was meeting before she entered the restaurant. They came to a street crossing, and Alexis sighed. A little red hand was flashing at her from the other side of the crosswalk. They would have to wait for the walk signal, and by then Alexis was sure Chloe would be gone, along with any chance of finding out who her boss was.

Alexis turned to say something to Bailey, but she was gone. Alexis looked up again and yelled.

"Bailey, no!"

Bailey hadn't noticed the flashing red hand. She had plowed right into the crosswalk and into the path of a bus!

Last Chances

A huge arm came out of nowhere and shoved Alexis away from the street. A second later, something heavy landed on top of her. She had no idea what had happened—there was just this incredibly painful worry deep in her chest.

Bailey! What had happened to her friend?

After half a minute, Alexis realized the pain in her chest wasn't just the worry. She couldn't breathe. *Chloe's boss has found out about us and knocked me down!*

Then she realized the man who'd shoved her back on the sidewalk was her father. He was sprawled next to her, clutching Bailey in his arms. He rolled off, and the three of them sat on the slushy sidewalk, staring wide eyed.

"Are you okay, Bailey?" Mr. Howell asked, out of breath.

"Um, yeah. I think so." Bailey's voice barely squeaked out. Alexis thought she sounded like a very small chipmunk.

"I came looking for you two. I'm glad I was here, too. That bus almost had your name on it, Bailey. It's a good thing we're leaving tomorrow. You girls don't need to go looking for any more trouble. Let me guess—you two were following a lead."

"Well, yes," said Alexis. "But Bailey just got excited, that's all! This investigation isn't dangerous, Dad, I promise!"

Mr. Howell scowled and pointed to the bruise on Alexis's cheek. He crossed his arms, waiting for her to explain her way out of that one. Her answer surprised him.

"It's okay, Dad. We've solved the case!"

"You have?"

"We have?" echoed Bailey. She was just as surprised as Mr. Howell.

"Yes! I almost forgot because of the whole bus thing, but didn't you hear what Chloe said to her boss just before we lost her?"

Bailey scrunched up her face, trying to remember. She shook her head. Mr. Howell was scratching his.

"Well, you two better get up to the room if you're going to have enough time to get ready for your party," said Mr. Howell. "Your mom's up there dancing out of her shoes. She's more excited than you are—her makeup's all over the place, and I think she has out five different curling irons, or straighteners, or something like that."

"Thanks, Dad. Come on, Bailey!"

Alexis towed Bailey toward the elevator. Once the doors closed, Bailey spoke up.

"So what did she say?" she asked.

"Shh!" Alexis whispered. She pointed to the three businessmen on the elevator. The doors opened on floors three and five, and eventually Alexis and Bailey were alone.

"So?" pressed Bailey.

"I can't believe you didn't hear her!" said Alexis.

"I was so worried about catching up to her that I wasn't really listening, Lexi. Now come on!"

"Okay, okay!" said Alexis. "There are two things. First of all, she mentioned permanent paint! It sounded like her boss was having a hard time washing it off of something!"

"Wow! So her boss really *is* the one sabotaging the reserve," said Bailey.

"Yes! Unless it's a really big coincidence, and you know how I feel about those."

"There's still a problem though," said Bailey. "We don't know who her boss *is*."

Alexis didn't stop smiling. The elevator doors

opened on their floor, and she pranced down the hall toward their room.

"I know, but do you know what else Chloe said?" Alexis asked. Bailey shook her head, jogging down the hall to catch up.

"She told her boss that his *tuxedo for the benefit* was in his room! Bailey! He's going to be at the party tonight! Even if we don't know who he is now, we'll definitely know by the end of the night! We just have to watch Chloe to find out who she's working for."

Alexis dug around in her bag for the room key.

"Come on! Let's call Jake and tell him the good news!"

Mrs. Howell was buzzing around the room like a queen bee. Alexis thought she might be more excited than the girls were about the party.

"Over here, ladies! Did you get dresses? Here, let me iron them for you." She swept the shopping bags out of Alexis's hand and headed toward the bedroom. Alexis picked up the phone and dialed the number for the reserve. Lisa picked up, but within a minute she had given the phone to Jake.

Alexis told him all about finding Chloe and that they were absolutely sure her boss was the one sabotaging the reserve.

"He'll be there tonight, Jake!" said Alexis. "We can

turn him in and get him to confess! Then the disasters will stop, and the government won't be able to take away your license!"

Silence filled the other end of the phone. Alexis was sure that Jake was speechless. He was probably amazed that they had solved the case in under a week.

"Um, Alexis?" Jake said after a minute or two. "I hate to break it to you, but we can't just go around accusing members of Tahoe's elite society of being criminals. If this guy really does have money—and it sounds like he does—he's not just going to confess to all of this. There's a reason he's sabotaging us, anyway. He's not going to just give up because some kids are on to him. No offense!" Jake sighed.

"You girls have done a great job, Alexis," Jake continued. "But we're going to need hard evidence if we're going to stop this guy."

"Okay, Jake," said Alexis. "See you in a few hours."

"Okay," said Jake. "Hey, let me know if you come up with anything else, okay?" It sounded like Jake felt sorry for them.

"Mmm-hmm," said Alexis. Then she hung up the phone.

Ugh! It was so unfair! They had worked so hard. How was it possible to be so close and so far away at the same time?

"He's right, you know," said Bailey. "We have to have evidence. This guy isn't going to roll over and admit his crimes to a couple of girls."

"I know!" Alexis said. She stomped her foot in frustration. "There *has* to be a way."

"Girls! Dresses are ready!" called Mrs. Howell.

For the next hour and a half, the girls allowed Mrs. Howell to dress them up as if they were Barbie dolls. She ignored them as they talked about the case and searched for ways to pin the sabotage on Chloe's boss.

"There's still the red paint," said Bailey as Mrs. Howell tugged a wrinkle out of her slip. "His hand should be red, right?"

"Yeah," said Alexis. "That's good, but it may not be enough. He could come up with a ton of reasons why his hand might have gotten paint on it."

Mrs. Howell had started working on Alexis's makeup, and it was really hard to think through the case with the makeup brushes tickling her face.

"Careful, Mom," Alexis said. "I don't want to look like a clown."

"Don't worry, hon," said Mrs. Howell. "No one will even be able to tell you're wearing any makeup. It's just a light blush, lip gloss, and a little bit of mascara to make your gorgeous eyes pop on camera. You two are filming the benefit for the documentary, right?"

"Yep!" Truthfully, Alexis had forgotten all about the documentary. She was glad her mother had mentioned it, but it also made her nervous. She would have to do two things at once tonight—finish filming the documentary *and* solidify their case against Chloe's boss. And she wasn't sure how she and Bailey would get both tasks done at the same time.

"Okay, now that you two are ready, I'm going to go finish fixing my own face," Mrs. Howell said with a smile.

"Let's go check our e-mail, Lexi, and see if the girls have worked any of their magic while we've been out today."

"You know if she could hear you, Elizabeth would say it's not magic!" Alexis said as she retrieved her mom's computer from the other room.

"You bet! Betty-boo would remind us that God cares about every detail of our lives and is always at work—even when we least expect it," Bailey said with a grin.

"Speaking of which, looks like everyone is signed on, including Betty-boo. We hit it at the right time."

Alexis: *Hi CCG! We're getting ready to go to a banquet with the celebrities.*

Elizabeth: *I've been praying for you all day. I sense that the Lord is going to break through some confusion tonight.*

Alexis: *Good! It's about time for us to leave, so it's almost like it's tonight or never! And we haven't failed a CCG case yet! I don't want this to be the first one.*

Elizabeth: *Jesus asked His disciples: "You of little faith. . .why did you doubt?" And I think that's the message He has for us today, too.*

Sydney: *Speaking of messages for today, I've been doing some pretty intensive work on the Internet.*

Alexis: *About what?*

Sydney: *I just have a feeling that developer who has been bugging Jake and Karen is involved in this in some way. The feeling wouldn't go away.*

Elizabeth: *That's exciting because God often works in our lives by giving us ideas that won't go away!*

McKenzie: *I've been thinking about the developer, too. If he's rich and he's used to having his way, well, it sounds like he's pretty ruthless. Sounds like he can only think about what he wants, not about what's best for the animals and people around the reserve. Those kinds of people can be pretty impulsive.*

Sydney: *Wait. You haven't heard what I did.*

Alexis: *Well, what did you do?*

Sydney: *I took the name of the company you gave us the other day, and I looked it up on the Internet. I thought maybe it would tell us the name of his assistant or secretary. Then we could see if that Chloe girl was his assistant. Assistants often do things like scheduling equipment—like snow-blowers or snowmobiles or whatever that thing was—for their bosses.*

McKenzie: *What did you find out?*

Sydney: *Nothing. From the website, that is.*

McKenzie: *Aww. You got our hopes up for nothing. . .not to mention Alexis and Bailey's.*

Sydney: *Wait a minute. You keep inter-rupting. I couldn't find the names of any of his staff people at his office, but I found the phone number. And I called it.*

Alexis: *Did you ask him if he'd been threatening anyone or committing acts of sabotage?*

Sydney: *No, silly. But I did ask if I could talk to his assistant. And I told the person who answered the phone, "Now what's her name?"*

Alexis: *And?...*

Sydney: *And your instincts are completely true! The assistant's name is Chloe Stevens!*

Alexis: *Chloe Stevens! Wow, so Bruce Benton is Chloe Stevens's boss!*

Kate: *I hate to throw a damper on things, but even if Chloe Stevens rented a snowmobile for her boss, how do you know that her boss is the spray-paint person?*

Alexis: *We haven't told you yet, but we heard Chloe talking on the phone earlier today. She told the lady at the store she was talking to her boss. And then she said something about his getting the permanent red paint off of his hands.*

Bailey suddenly spoke up. "Uh, Lexi, I just realized something. That was on another call. She'd hung up from her call with Benton and was talking on the phone again when she said that."

Alexis sat stumped for a moment. *Bailey's right! We don't know for sure that she was talking to Benton again.*

After she got her breath back from the surprise, she typed this new information onto the screen for the girls to read.

McKenzie: *So all we really know is that she was telling someone how to get red paint off his or her hands, right? We don't even know it was a man.*

Alexis: *Yeah, her tone of voice hadn't changed much, so I just assumed she was still talking to her boss. But it might not have been. What are we going to do? Any suggestions?*

Sydney: *Can you shadow Chloe tonight? Watch her and see who she talks to. See if any of the men have a red hand.*

McKenzie: *Will you have time to keep on her trail?*

Alexis: *I don't know. I have to work on filming the event and filming Bailey interviewing people.*

Kate: *Too bad you can't pull a James Bond and plant some sort of monitoring device on her.*

Alexis: *Kate, you're brilliant! I can go James Bond on her. I forgot about the lapel mic! It's actually to put on Bailey while I'm taping her. She talks into the lapel mic, and I can receive it through a device in my ear, even if I'm in another room. If I could plant the mic on Chloe, I could hear everything she says.*

Elizabeth: *But wait, you wouldn't be able to see the men or their hands.*

Kate: *Too bad you don't have a tiny video bug you could plant on her purse or dress and see the hands of the men she talks to.*

Sydney: *I'm still thinking about this Bruce Benton guy. If he's the one trying to destroy the animal reserve, do you think he'll try to ruin the event tonight? Could you plant the mic on him? Then you could hear if he's up to something.*

Alexis: *I don't see how I could. Bailey's sitting here and just said she doesn't see how we could, either.*

McKenzie: *And what if he's not the man with the red hand? You could be concentrating on him and wouldn't even realize if anyone*

*is popping Jake with another punch or
shooting another BB gun—or worse. . . .*

Elizabeth: *Maybe that's what you should do
with the lapel mic. Maybe you should put
it on Jake where no one can see it. That way
if anyone threatens him or does anything
else, you'll hear it.*

Alexis: *Brilliant idea, Elizabeth. I hope no
one harms Jake, but he's the one most likely
to have someone bother him. And we can
only plant the bug well on someone who
knows we're doing it. I'm sure he'll let us.*

Sydney: *Well, also keep an eye on Bruce Benton. . . .*

McKenzie: *And Chloe Stevens!*

Alexis: *We need a few more of you here on
site with us! We've gotta run if we want to
get hold of Jake before the benefit starts.*

Elizabeth: *Okay. Check in tonight, and let us
know what happened since you don't have
cell phones with you. And we'll all
be praying that God gives you wisdom,
understanding, and eyes that can
see everything!*

Alexis and Bailey were ecstatic. Alexis wasted no

time in pounding the number to the reserve into the hotel phone. She hoped that Karen and Jake hadn't left yet.

"Yes?" a voice answered.

It was Jake, and he sounded like he was in a hurry.

"Hey, Jake, it's Alexis. Can you guys drop by our room when you get to the hotel? We'd like to put a microphone on you for the evening, if that's okay. It won't take long."

"A mic?"

"Yes, we'll explain later, but we think it will help us catch whoever is trying to ruin the reserve," Alexis said.

"Yeah, yeah—sure. We'll be there in half an hour. What room?" After Jake jotted down the room number, he quickly hung up.

"He's going to do it?" asked Bailey.

"Yep!" Alexis said. "He sounded a little agitated though. I wonder if something else happened."

Mrs. Howell came into the front room carrying the girl's miniature purses. Bailey's was silver and went beautifully with her sapphire-blue dress and silver heels. Alexis's purse was the same color as her dress—a light peach that looked good with her pale skin and dark hair.

"I put the lip glosses in there for you," said Mrs. Howell. "You can borrow them for the evening in case you want to refresh."

"Thanks, Mom," said Alexis. She doubted that she would reapply the lip gloss, because she hardly ever wore the stuff. This one matched the color of her dress perfectly, though, and went great with her blue eyes, so maybe she would try it.

Before long, someone knocked on the door. Bailey rushed to open it, and Misty Marks swept into the room trailing her long, white dress behind her. Feathers ran from one of her shoulders down the back of the dress and all the way to the train, which rested on the floor. Her outfit was stunning.

Right away Alexis realized that she had forgotten to mention Misty Marks to her mother. Mrs. Howell stood in the middle of the room touching her hair absentmindedly with her mouth hanging open.

"You girls look absolutely gorgeous!" chimed Misty. She glided over to Mrs. Howell and introduced herself. Alexis was glad Misty was there to keep her mother busy while she and Bailey hooked up Jake, who looked like he'd rather be in one of his flannel shirts than the rented tuxedo he wore.

Alexis could tell that something was bothering him.

His face—bruised pretty badly from the punch he'd taken the day before—was covered with worry.

"What's wrong, Jake?" Alexis asked as Bailey untangled the cord on the lapel mic.

"What? Oh, nothing, nothing," said Jake. "Everything's fine. Do you really think this will work?"

"Well, it's a long shot, but if anyone suspicious approaches you or threatens you tonight, we'll get it all on tape, and I'll hear it through the receiver," said Alexis.

"Mmm," was all Jake said. His face darkened even more.

"Is there something you're not telling us, Jake?" asked Alexis. "We can't help if you keep us in the dark, you know."

Alexis and Bailey faced the large man in front of them with their hands on their hips. That made him smile.

"Okay, okay," Jake said. "You mentioned threats? Well, I received one just before we left the reserve to come over here. That's why I was so short with you on the phone. Look, it's right here."

Jake reached into the inside pocket of his tux and pulled out a folded letter. Alexis recognized it at once as another message glued together out of resort brochures. The glue was still fresh. Alexis's fingers stuck to the letter in the damp places. She and Bailey stared at the single sentence with wide eyes.

Tonight's your last chance.

Thank You, James Bond

Bailey and Alexis followed Jake and Misty through the hotel and into the gigantic ballroom. They were early, so the room was empty except for a few waiters here and there, and Karen. She was putting some animals in their cages in places that would be highlighted throughout the evening.

Karen's dress was bright red, matching her lipstick. When the girls reached her near the stage, Alexis saw that Bubbles had come to the party as well. He was wearing a brand-new collar that matched Karen's dress.

"The other animals will stay in their cages," said Karen as she hugged the girls. "Bubbles is used to people, and he's great at getting donations! All I have to do is walk around with him and tell his story every time someone asks about him!"

Alexis looked up onto the stage and saw two large golden cages. In each cage sat a golden eagle—the largest in the eagle family. Their feathers were a golden brown, and their eyes sparkled bronze. One of the creatures spread his wings, and Alexis understood why the cages were so large. The bird's wingspan was six feet across!

"They're so majestic!" squealed Bailey. "They look like gorgeous statues!"

"This is Kelly and that one's Ben," said Karen. "They were shot last year. We're hoping to release them as soon as it warms up."

"They're a surprise!" squeaked Misty. "The curtains will be closed most of the night. We'll open them just before Jake's speech and let people ogle the birds before we ask for their money!"

Misty chuckled. The girls could tell she was having a blast, and the party hadn't even started yet!

Jake took the girls to a prime table right in front of the stage. Their names were scrawled in gold on two beautiful place settings. Alexis had never felt like a princess before, but she was pretty sure that this was what it would feel like.

"You girls are free to mingle all night," said Jake. "Film anything and anyone. Even the movie stars. They know there'll be cameras. Here—these will keep anyone from thinking you're in the wrong place or giving you a hard time."

Jake pulled two badges out of his pocket and handed one each to Alexis and Bailey. They were press passes.

"You don't have to wear them," he said. "I know they won't match the dresses. If you want, you can just keep them with you in case anyone gets nosy about your camera."

"Thanks, Jake!" said Alexis. "Be sure to turn on your microphone before the party starts."

"I will. Look—I don't expect anything to happen, but if you hear or see anything fishy, I want you to notify one of the police officers who will be on duty, all right? No being the hero?"

It was clear that Jake was still thinking about the threat he'd received. He was more than a little edgy.

"Gotcha," said Alexis and Bailey together.

Not long afterwards, music began playing. Alexis noticed a DJ near the back of the room. People began streaming into the ballroom, and in no time the party was in full swing. It was hard not to be dazzled by all the stars. A couple of times when they spotted a favorite, they jabbed each other and whispered excitedly. The girls found they really had to focus to keep their mission in mind.

"First let's just do general taping," Alexis suggested. "We'll go around taping the event and people, and decide which stars we want to talk to later."

"What about Chloe?" Bailey asked.

"We'll look for her while we're wandering around and getting an overview. That's why I just want to start filming and wandering—that will give us an excuse to go around looking for her."

"Then we can follow her until we see who her boss is?"

"Yes, that's what I was thinking," Alexis said. "Or even better, I hope she'll arrive with him, so we get that figured out right away."

"I wonder if she knows how he got the red paint," Bailey said. "I wonder if she's in on it, too."

"I don't know. I guess we'll just have to wait and see."

"What are we going to do when we see her with her boss?" Bailey asked.

"Well, first of all, let's get close and see if his hand is red with the spray paint. Then we're going to have to come up with some way to see if we can get some evidence to confront him with.

"I hate to say this," said Alexis, "but I actually hope this guy threatens Jake to his face. I mean, I don't want him to hurt him, but if we could get a threat on tape, it would be something to take to the police. . . . Bailey?"

Alexis turned and saw that Bailey had wandered

off. She was back at their table chatting away with yet another Oscar winner. Alexis shrugged and kept walking lazily through the crowd. To an outsider, it would look like she was simply listening to the easy party conversations going on all over the room. In reality, though, she was only listening to one person—Jake.

The earpiece in Alexis's ear caught a signal from his microphone and allowed her to hear everything. She figured it looked pretty natural for a camera operator to have an earpiece. At best, she just looked like she was listening to a director in the other room. At worst, she just looked like she had an earpiece for a cell phone in.

She was surprised to find that she could actually hear the other people talking to Jake as well. Alexis had been unsure if the mic would pick them up, but it did. Now all she had to do was wait for the *right person* to talk to Jake.

As if on cue, Alexis saw Chloe—the red-haired assistant—waltz through the door. She was in a beautiful, brown, floor-length gown, but her face looked the same as usual—grumpy. If Alexis was right, Chloe was not in the mood for a party.

And she was alone.

Alexis's high hopes plummeted. She had been so sure that Chloe's boss would arrive with her. Now, though, she realized that had been a silly thing to be sure of. They had never seen Chloe with her boss, so why should this party be any different?

Alexis left her video camera at the table so she wouldn't be conspicuous and followed Chloe around. She watched the woman from a distance and kept track of every man she talked to. As soon as Chloe finished a conversation, Alexis would move in and do what she could to check the man's left hand for red paint.

She had to get pretty creative. Some of the men made it easy by waving to her with their left hands. Other times, she had to introduce herself and offer a hand to shake—the left one. She knew this made her look clumsy and naive, but it worked. Most people simply smiled at her mistake and shook her left hand anyway.

Soon it felt as if she had talked to every person in the room. She wasn't used to high heels, so her feet were beginning to hurt. Alexis returned to the table and found Bailey messing with the video camera.

"I got some great footage of the guests!" Bailey said as Alexis sat down. "Now I have it all set up to tape Jake's speech. Have you met anyone cool?"

Bailey went into detail about all the stars she had met and gotten autographs from, but Alexis didn't hear her. Misty was on the stage in front of the red curtain. She had a microphone and was getting ready to introduce Jake and the eagles.

But that wasn't what caught her eye. She had just seen Jake go backstage—and he hadn't gone alone.

Seconds after he disappeared behind the side of the curtain, another man followed. Alexis didn't see his face, but as the man moved the curtain back into place after himself, she saw the palm of his left hand.

It was red.

"Bailey, I'll be right back!" Alexis said. "Do me a favor and start filming now, will you?"

"But it doesn't look like anything's happening yet."

"I know, but trust me! Just start taping!" Alexis took off across the front of the room to the stairs at the side of the stage. The boy in charge of opening the curtain was bobbing his head to whatever song was playing on his iPod. He didn't even see her pass by.

At the bottom of the stairs, Alexis almost took off her heels, but she decided not to. Instead she tiptoed up the staircase as quietly as possible. She could hear the conversation in her earpiece before she saw Jake. Whoever was talking to him sounded angry, but Jake was furious. Alexis poked her head around a pillar and saw the two men nose to nose between the eagle cages.

"This is it, Bruce! I mean it!" Jake whispered.

"What do you mean, this is it?" said Bruce calmly. "You don't think I'll really just let you walk away from this idea, do you?"

"Are you threatening me?" asked Jake.

"That's up to you, Jake." Bruce was growling now. "Take this deal. I want your land, and I'm going to get it one way or another. This is your last chance to sell it. You can announce it here!"

"And if I don't?"

"Well, as you've learned, accidents happen," Bruce said. "Even accidents with kerosene spilled over from heaters in the barn and fires erupting. I wouldn't want to be you and hear the cries of injured animals. . . ."

Alexis gasped! Sydney had been right! Bruce Benton was the man who'd been trying to make Jake abandon the animal reserve.

And now he was going to burn down the reserve if Alexis didn't act quickly!

Surprise, Surprise

Jake pulled a piece of paper out of his front pocket.

"You sent this, didn't you?" Jake asked, waving the paper in Bruce's face. Alexis recognized it as the latest threat letter. Bruce didn't answer, but a large smile spread across his wide jaw.

"You did all of this! You painted my barn? You poisoned my coyotes and woke up a hibernating bear? You shot a kid with a BB gun? Bruce—you *hit me in the face!*"

Jake was furious now. If it hadn't been for the music outside, Alexis was sure that everyone would be able to hear this.

That was it! Everyone *needed* to hear this! It was all the evidence they needed to stop Bruce Benton. The music stopped, and Misty's voice drifted over the ballroom. Alexis had an idea.

She ran back into the ballroom, finally tossing off her heels as she leaped down the stairs. Alexis made straight for the DJ's booth in the back. The young man running it looked at her bare feet and raised his eyebrows. Alexis ignored him.

"Jake needs another microphone," she said. She was shocked when he simply nodded and handed her a cordless microphone.

"It's on," he said. "You just have to push that button to unmute it."

"Thanks!" Alexis said.

In a matter of moments, she was sliding through the curtains again.

"You're being stupid, Jake! We're talking about millions of dollars!" Bruce Benton nearly shouted.

Alexis took the earpiece out of her ear and put it up to the microphone. She propped it there with one hand. Then she took a deep breath, pushed the mute button, and tucked the microphone a little behind her body, where her skirt would partially hide it.

"So you admit you're the one who's been hurting the animals and trying to ruin the reserve?" Alex called out evenly from several yards away.

Bruce Benton turned on his heels with alarm. . . until he saw it was only a young girl standing there. He didn't even notice the mic she held.

"So what if I did?" Bruce Benton said with a sneer.

"It's my word against old Jakey-boy's here. And I have more money. . . . Are the police going to believe an animal nut or a fine, upstanding businessman?

"Yeah," he said, looking at Jake. "That's a great angle. We'll tell 'em this animal nut has gone nuts and is causing his own attempts at sabotage. Going crazy. Trying to get insurance money. . ."

"No one will ever believe that!" Jake exclaimed.

"Sure they will. It's your word against mine. No one will listen to a little girl like this, so it's just your word against. . . Hey, what are you doing?"

While Benton had been talking, Alexis had slowly edged over to the curtains and started to pull the ropes to open them. Sometime during Benton's speech, Misty had stopped talking.

"What's going on here?"

Now with the curtains open, Bruce Benton could hear what he hadn't heard behind the curtains—his voice booming over the room's sound-system speakers, through Alexis's microphone.

News reporters dashed from the back of the room toward the stage, but a police officer who'd been stationed in the back of the room beat them. Quietly, the officer stepped up to the stage, "Mr. Benton, we've heard your whole conversation there, sir. You're under arrest for willfully harming animals and destroying property. You have the right to remain silent, sir. Anything you say can be used against you in a court of law. . . ."

Alexis's eyes met those of Bailey's at the head table, and both girls exchanged smiles of pure glee.

●—●—●

The next morning, Alexis and Bailey barely made it to the slopes in time for Angelo's race. They had stayed out so late that they had slept right through the hotel alarm. As a result, both of them were wearing beanie caps shoved low over their leftover curly hairdos from the party.

With Bruce's arrest, Jake and Karen had told the group about the sabotage attempts on the animal reserve.

And after the grand unveiling of what Bruce Benton had been doing, Karen and Jake had told the whole room about Alexis, Bailey, and the other Camp Club Girls solving the mystery. When they told the room about Alexis and Bailey doing the documentary, stars had literally lined up in the room, eager to help the girls by saying a few words to their camera about the reserve and why they supported it.

With all the excitement, some of the tightest of fists had opened to spur a flood of donations. Everyone attending was so inspired that they all gave something.

Even the DJ slipped a twenty-dollar bill sheepishly into the donation bin. Alexis and Bailey had been blown away by the selfless giving. Karen had called that morning to tell them that they had raised enough to build an animal hospital and hire on-site veterinarian help.

Now as they stood outside in the bright sunshine, Alexis took a deep breath. A unique fragrance drifted in on the cold air. It was the smell of snow—something that Alexis had never noticed before—and it made her smile.

"Look! There's Angelo!" Bailey was standing on the top of a picnic table to get a good look at the race course. Alexis jumped up beside her and squinted into the sun. It was a beautiful day, and the snow was as bright as a mirror reflecting the sun.

"Where?" asked Alexis.

"Up at the start!" said Bailey. "He's wearing his green jacket and a bright yellow helmet."

"I see him! Go, Angelo!" Alexis shouted.

Within minutes, the horn sounded, and Angelo took off down the mountain. His guide stayed well ahead of him, and the way Angelo skied made it look like he'd been born to fly over the snow. He weaved in and out of the red and blue flags, shaving so close to them he made the crowd gasp.

"You would never know he was blind if you didn't know him," said Alexis. She was amazed. When she had first met Angelo, she remembered feeling sorry for him and a bit protective. This week had taught her a lot of things though, and one of them was that people and things that seem helpless almost never are. In fact, without Angelo they might not have solved this case. . . and she might have been eaten by a cranky bear. It had been him, after all, who pulled her back onto the snowmobile when she fell off.

Within minutes, the race was over. Angelo had beaten his opponent by a wide margin, and Alexis and Bailey ran to meet him.

"Angelo! That was amazing!" said the girls together.

"You totally toasted that guy!" said Bailey.

"Did I? I thought it felt like I was alone up front," Angelo said, but Alexis could tell by his smile that he knew exactly how badly he had beaten his opponent. "That was the semifinals. This afternoon I'll race for first place!"

"That's awesome, Angelo!" said Alexis. "I wish we could stay to see it, but you'll have to e-mail me. We have to leave after lunch. Bailey flies out from Sacramento tomorrow morning, so we have to get home tonight."

"I'll miss you," said Angelo, "but I'll send you pictures. My mom's watching."

Angelo pointed over to the stands, and Alexis and Bailey saw a beautiful woman waving at them. She looked just like Angelo, only prettier.

"I wanted to thank you two," said Angelo. "I wouldn't have been able to race without you. I had a blast yesterday practicing, too. You really made this vacation great. It started off awful. . .but most of that was probably my bad attitude."

"Don't mention it," said Alexis. "You taught me a lot, too. I'll never assume that a 'disability' makes someone need me. I think I needed you more than you needed me anyway!"

"I *did* save your life, I guess," laughed Angelo.

"Hey," Angelo said, looking serious. "Remember the day we met?"

"When I hit you in the head?" said Bailey.

"No, the next day, just over there on that bench." The girls nodded. "Well, you asked me what I liked to 'observe,' and I was really rude. I never answered you."

Alexis and Bailey looked puzzled.

"You see," continued Angelo, "I observe with all of my other senses. That day I was paying particular attention to the smell of snow."

"The smell of snow?" asked Bailey.

"Yep!" said Angelo. "Try it sometime, and think of me."

Bailey and Alexis each gave Angelo a hug and waved good-bye to his mother. Within an hour they had eaten and were back in the car with Alexis's family driving Highway 89 back down toward the Valley and Sacramento.

In the back of the car, Bailey and Alexis had the laptop open and earphones on. They were editing tape for their documentary, and they were surprised to see how much it looked like a suspense movie. They had tons of information about the animals on the reserve, but they had also documented the reserve's struggle against Bruce. Bailey had taped a lot during the party, and she had caught Bruce's confession, too.

The final two minutes of film were a huge surprise.

"Did you tape this?" Alexis asked Bailey.

"No," she answered. "I thought you had."

The girls sat in silence and watched. It was a close-up of Misty Marks, famous actress, speaking directly into the camera.

"The goal of the Tahoe Animal Reserve is simple," she was saying. "Watch over those who cannot watch over themselves. This applies to our animals, but it applies to our everyday interactions as well. Everywhere we go, there are people who *need*. Look around you. Notice the needs and fill them when you can. The smallest good can fill the largest gap."

Misty smiled broadly into the camera.

"Thank you, Camp Club Girls, for filling our gap. We are forever grateful."

Alexis couldn't see the screen anymore. The tears in her eyes were getting in the way. She wiped at them with the back of her hand and turned to Bailey who was smiling through her own tears.

As Alexis watched the Jeffrey pines race by outside the window, she said a silent prayer: *Thank You so much, God. Thanks for helping us. Thanks for helping these people. Please help me to always see the little gaps that I can help fill in people's lives—even when they look too small to be important.*

Alexis looked back at the screen. She had never been so excited about a project in her life. She knew this documentary would be a winner—whether it made it on the Discovery Channel or not.

Want **MORE** of the Camp Club Girls?

Visit them online at www.campclubgirls.com

☆ **GET THE 411 ON YOUR FAVORITE CAMP CLUB GIRL!**

☆ **PRINT YOUR OWN BOOKMARK TO USE IN YOUR FAVORITE BOOK!**

☆ **GET THE SCOOP ON UPCOMING ADVENTURES**

☆ **CHECK OUT THE NEW CAMP CLUB GIRLS NEWSLETTER— CAMPFIRE STORIES!**

Follow Your Favorite Camp Club Girls and Help Crack the Case

Check Off the Books as You Solve Each Mystery

Available Wherever Books Are Sold